LIFE ON THE NILE

Janice Elliott
LIFE ON THE NILE

Hodder & Stoughton
LONDON SYDNEY AUCKLAND TORONTO

British Library Cataloguing in Publication Data
Elliott, Janice, *1931–*
    Life on the Nile.
    I. Title
    823′.914[F]

ISBN 0-340-49595-2

First published in Great Britain 1989

Published by Hodder and Stoughton,
a division of Hodder and Stoughton Ltd,
Mill Road, Dunton Green, Sevenoaks, Kent TN13 2YA.
Editorial Office: 47 Bedford Square, London WC1B 3DP.

Typeset by Hewer Text Composition Services, Edinburgh.
Printed in Great Britain by St Edmundsbury Press, Bury St Edmunds, Suffolk.

For Chaim Raphael

1

Here they were then, in Cairo, in the splendid hotel: fountains, palms, gravel raked, blue-eyed pool, the taped call to prayer of the muezzin, so enormously amplified the city seemed to shout. On the balcony Charlotte simply stood, her face raised to the sun, the ache drained from her bones.

The evening before when they arrived, tipped, it felt, over the disc of the earth from damp northern chill, she had stepped from the plane into a night like fur. Coming in to land, she had had the feeling of a single, dark wave turning lazily on the shore below, the skirts of Africa. And of the continent stretched out unimaginably south. She had felt a stronger pull than she had ever known before, while behind her, north, life, cares, past, slackened.

Not quite her father's death, that could not be shrugged off. Well, we grow older, Charlotte thought. That is to say, we reach quite suddenly the point at which we no longer believe that the future is boundless, that those we love are immortal.

She turned back into the room where Leo still lay in a twist of sheet. Leo. Lion. That hair colour that never turns entirely grey but fades to a paler gold. Time sucks out the light.

She knelt to kiss him.

'What's this then?' Leo yawned with a grin.

'Nothing really.'

Charlotte could not have explained the odd little intimation of something like fear. The exact counterbalance to joy. Even as they touched down she had felt it. A message delivered. Along with exhilaration, a warning not yet interpreted.

'Father always wanted to come, you know. From childhood. It was the passion of his life, all he ever had really.

7

Phoebe's letters did that. The aunt who died here.' Was killed.

'Why didn't he?'

'Perhaps he couldn't bear to. By the time he was old enough she was dead. Then he wasn't what you'd call an adventuring man, was he? I suppose he preferred to keep it intact, not to measure it against reality – his dream of Egypt. Poor Father.'

Leo was dressed.

'Aren't we due to be somewhere? Hal Douglas's?'

'Not till tonight.'

'Thank God. What time is it?'

'After lunch. Which we haven't had.'

Leo put his hands on her shoulders.

'Something up? Tired?'

Charlotte shook her head and turned to him.

'You?'

Leo laughed.

'I'm fine. Feel my heart. Beating.'

'Yes.'

'And I'm starving. Come on. Let's go down.'

'I'm sorry. What did you say?'

Charlotte had wandered from the party into the garden of the villa. She walked down the path between the pale roses and looked back at the lighted room as one standing on a beach might observe a ship close inshore.

There were passengers grouped within the rectangles of light, the women in their party dresses, all those mouths moving behind glass, the glasses, the flowers, the women, their faces tipped up like flowers to the men.

And then one of Hal Douglas's hired help – the Nubian giant in his galabiya – cut across the picture. And when he had passed the tide of the party left Leo's figure momentarily stranded. Charlotte could see him clearly but he, peering from the light into the darkness, was blind. He could not make her out.

'Do you like Egypt?'

Not a ghost. Egyptian? Hard to tell if he had an accent until he spoke again. Short. By the light of the moon and the lamp around which small moths clustered, she could make out a silk sheen to his suit, a lustre to his starling-black hair. The musky scent she had imagined to be flowers might be his, more like a woman's perfume than aftershave.

'I'm sorry, that's a foolish question. The Egyptians never stop asking: do you like my beloved country? As no doubt you have discovered.'

'No. I've only been here a few hours. My name's Charlotte Hamp.'

'Mine is Masoud Suleiman. And your husband?'

'He's inside there. The tall one.'

'Ah, yes.'

The man had been in the garden longer than she, his night-eyes were sharper.

'Your ring – a scarab.'

'Yes. I bought it in the hotel tonight. Silly, I suppose. Probably made in Birmingham or Hong Kong.'

'No.' He held her hand up with the tips of his fingers. 'Not bad quality at all.'

'I've forgotten. A creation myth?'

'One of many. In Egypt there is never a single explanation for anything. That at least has not changed. The version I prefer is that of the lotus. From the lotus came the scarab beetle, from the beetle the boy who wept and created mankind.'

'That's beautiful.'

A plane coming into Heliopolis from the south ripped the sky, deafening. The air shook.

'I'm sorry. What did you say?'

'The beauty. That you mustn't be dazzled.'

'Why not?'

They were walking slowly back up the path towards the lighted room, paused by a stone tank in which dozed a phosphorescent fish.

'If I want to be?'

9

'Then by all means, yes. It depends how much you wish to understand.'

Charlotte nodded. In the frame of light she could see Leo between two women. Something they said made him laugh. He flung back his head. He looked like an old lion between young, bright birds. One laid a tiny, varnished claw on his forearm.

'Oh, I'm not sure I want to understand. If I could. This is a holiday for me. I'm just a camp follower. Leo's doing the work.'

'Of course. But if you should change your mind – my card. My address here and at Aswan.'

'Thank you.'

Back in the room the party had passed its crescendo. Many had left. The rest had split into small groups, mostly sitting down. Leo's birds had flown away and he was lounging on the fringe of a half-circle gathered around Hal Douglas. He flung out an arm in Charlotte's direction and she allowed her hand to rest lightly on his shoulder.

Hal Douglas was saying: 'A couple of Libyan missiles on the Aswan dam and Egypt's out of the game. When the Gulf business was on the rest of the Arab states kissed and made up but that was because they needed the Egyptian army. Egypt's hungry and that suits the Fundamentalists. Mubarak goes to bed with the States and there's a bus to Tel Aviv from outside the Nile Hilton. You knew that, Charlie?'

Charlotte shook her head.

'Ask Max Stiller. Eh, Max?'

'Not a journey I would choose to take.'

Charlotte turned to the last speaker. She had not noticed him before. Elderly, he sat on a cane chair in the corner. He had an almost bald pate, a fluff of white hair and thick lenses in his spectacles which gave him an air of watching. Laughing perhaps? Of being outside, at least. Jewish? He was sipping mineral water, raised his glass to Charlotte but before she could cross the white carpet to speak to him Hal was organising them all into going out for dinner.

Cars were called, taxis for the overflow and Charlotte found herself pressed between Leo and Hal as the caravan bumped from the city streets to a road that seemed half made, that lacking lights or any direction she could make out, could surely be going nowhere, except perhaps deeper into the darkness.

Then there was light again and they seemed to be in the suburbs. A restaurant? A hotel? Charlotte shivered in her silk dress: it seemed colder here. The scrunch of tyres on gravel, a thin scent in the air – oleander?

'Charlie, here. Hey, where's Max? Anyone seen Max?'

Hal was clearly known here. They were conducted between screens of fretted wood up a shallow flight of stairs. Tables had been pushed together. They were expected.

By the time Charlotte had served herself, not hungry, uncertain what to choose from the hot and cold buffet, she took the only place left. Leo had been seized by the women again. The table was dimly lit but Charlotte could see that while one was young, the other of the varnished claws forking now at the rice, only appeared so. Bird-thin, she wore a European-style dress the colour of kingfisher-blue and on her head a satin cap seeded with tiny pearls. From it a sleek feather swept downwards. Her fingers flashed with jewels and she ate in small pounces, talking a great deal. Leo was nodding his big head and smiling, turning now and then to the young woman at his other side, dressed in a simple brown kaftan.

Many had arrived a little drunk and the noise was loudest at Hal Douglas's end of the table.

Hal raised his glass.

'Hey, Charlie, all right?'

'Fine.'

'Allow me to fill your glass. Ptolemy is not too bad, I believe. If you prefer it I am sure we could order French. At a price.' Max Stiller finished pouring. 'You have been here before?'

11

'Egypt?'

'The Mena House.'

'Oh, no. I didn't know where we were. I've heard of it. I'm sorry. I'm Charlotte Hamp.'

'Max Stiller.'

Charlotte smiled. Nice man? Frog face. He seemed not to be eating. He noticed her gaze, shrugged, dismissed the matter of eating.

'It has been, as they say, done over for the tourists. But then who would have believed a bus across Sinai? It used to take forty years.' While Charlotte ate, Max fiddled with a roll, crumbled it but did not eat. 'You're on Hal Douglas's spree then?'

'My husband is. I'm tagging along.'

'I doubt that?'

She looked up at him. Behind the pebble spectacles it was hard to catch his expression but Charlotte felt it to be benevolent.

'Well, there was something I hoped to do. I'll see. You know Hal well?'

'Who knows Hal? I have never met a man who had so many acquaintances. The Americans – they are the modern Romans, don't you think? Strutting about the world. Brutal and sanctimonious.' Max smiled wickedly. 'Though don't mistake me. Many of my best friends are Americans. Tell me, would you like some air?'

Charlotte had pushed aside her own plate. There were shrieks of laughter from the other end of the table.

'Yes, that would be lovely.'

Charlotte followed. Away from the bright, noisy table she nearly missed another flight of steps. She was aware of the latticed screens, areas of darkness.

'Tell me, who is that woman in the blue dress?'

'Blue? Oh yes. Nina Fahmi. French, born in the Lebanon, buried I forget how many husbands, married an Egyptian. She was in with the crowd who hung round Farouk. She knew the Sadats too. Ask her to take you to the shop where Madame

12

Sadat buys her clothes. If you have time. Nina's a woman who survives revolutions. Well, there we are.'

A few yards into the garden, Max stood back, pleased with himself at having surprised her.

'The Pyramids! I hadn't realised they were so close.'

'You're seeing them at their best. Ah, the son et lumière's finishing or there's a power failure.'

Even as they watched there was something like a blink and the golden pyramids were black. As the light was withdrawn they seemed larger, waiting.

'Shall we sit down? You're not too cold?'

'No. It's sheltered here.'

His thick-lensed spectacles gleamed by the light of the garden lamp. The folded loungers round the pool dozed, waiting for the day. Max had chosen a white-painted iron chair. His feet hardly touched the ground. A light breeze ruffled the surface of the turquoise swimming-pool, setting a child's orange beach-ball bobbing. A tall figure crossed the corner of the garden, carrying a tray. He called in the harsh-sounding language to someone unseen. Charlotte thought, after Europe there is no starting-point here, I cannot enter the picture. I cannot even see the picture.

'So what is it Charlotte Hamp hopes to do in Egypt?'

Charlotte had almost forgotten the presence of the little man. This was an evening of odd conversations in gardens.

'Not much. Well, it might be. I'm a publisher's reader. Freelance. Some family letters and scraps of a journal came my way – my own family, I mean. You know *Letters from Egypt*? Nothing as solid as that. Phoebe Duncan – she was much later than Lucy Duff Gordon but there might just be a book. If there was a chance I thought I'd ask around a bit. Luxor and Aswan. There was a tragedy and some hint of scandal. A daughter called Pansy. It's just possible she's still alive. And you? What are you doing here?'

'A Jew in Egypt?'

Was he laughing?

'Oh, no. I didn't mean – '

13

'Of course not. The truth is, I am a poor sort of Jew but a greedy traveller. I first came to Egypt in search of Joseph. Before the many troubles. Now it is possible again, for the moment. I am putting off completing the book by pretending that it is necessary to come again. Well, who could refuse the bounty of Hal Douglas and the American Centre in Cairo?'

'Do you know who else is coming?'

'I saw a list somewhere,' Max said. 'Let me think. A couple of writers, I think, package holiday people, an actress, a doctor, a few academics. No, I've forgotten. Most of them haven't arrived yet. A suspicious number of Hal's friends. I wonder whose bounty it really is. It suits me very well, anyway. I was on my way to Jerusalem.'

Charlotte reached into her bag for a cigarette.

'So you're cultural, not trade.'

'Officially.'

'Leo's a travel writer so I suppose we're in the middle.'

They heard Hal's back-slapping laugh from within.

Charlotte smiled. 'Is it true what Hal says – the Americans are propping up Egypt? Economically, I mean.'

'Ah yes, the American fiefdom. Extendeth to the Children of Israel and Allah alike.'

'Leo's a very amateur archaeologist too. I think that's his real passion, or he wishes it could be.'

'You think?'

Charlotte paused in lighting her cigarette. A sharp question put mildly.

'You know, I've never really thought about it but it's the one thing he never discusses. Or not much. A sort of secret life. I suppose we all have something like that. He's so open otherwise. I think in a funny way he's a very innocent person. Do you know what I mean?'

Did Max nod in the darkness? He said: 'So we're all looking for something. I for Joseph, your husband for his secrets, you for your lady of the letters.' His tone was light.

A comfortable silence.

14

Charlotte said: 'Anyway, he's known Hal for years. I've met him in England. So here we are.'

'And I am glad.'

'Thank you.'

'Charlotte? Charlie? What the hell are you doing out there?'

Charlotte laughed.

'I think we're wanted.' She paused for a moment before going in. 'Oh, I meant to ask. Do you know someone called Suleiman? Soleiman? He was at Hal's party but he doesn't seem to have come on.'

'Ah, yes. Masoud. A fixer, you might say. Al-Azhar University and the Sorbonne. Or so he claims. The al-Azhar part is probably true. One story is that his family came from Gurna – the village in the Valley of the Kings, which means they were probably tomb-robbers. Did he try to sell you anything?'

'Not exactly. He gave me his card.'

'He could be helpful. But pay only on delivery.'

'I'll remember that.'

In the car going back to the Cairo Marriott, Hal slipped his arm through Charlotte's. The streets were empty. The houses that might once have been beautiful looked dusty and closed as though their inhabitants had fled from some catastrophe. If there was life here there was no sign of it. Some appeared to be merely façades.

Hal said: 'You've got to see the City of the Dead, Charlie. You'd never believe it.'

Charlotte felt a chill (a premonition? More like something she remembered or already knew). Leo was sitting on the jump-seat opposite. She wanted to take his warm hands in hers.

'The Mameluke Cemetery?' Leo said.

Hal nodded.

'On the airport road. The Ministry of Tourism discourages visitors. The press in particular. Officially there is no poverty in Egypt but that's where they live – in the tombs. Off the garbage of Cairo.'

'We won't have time, will we?' Charlotte said. She was trying to recall the passage in Phoebe's journal:

> Alex tells me that in 1916 in preparation for the Battle for
> Sinai, such was the terrible state of the people in Aswan,
> cameleers were recruited from old men and boys in exchange
> for a little silver, a handful of dates and poor onions.

There was more on the same subject, later. Phoebe's observations – she could only just have arrived – on the apparent absence of beggars, at least of the desperate Indian sort. Something Alex said, or it might have been later, her friend Nayra, about the inevitable repercussions of press-ganging the starving to fight the Turks.

'The thing about the Egyptians,' Hal was saying, 'is that they love conspiracy, mystery. It makes them hell to deal with. They look like hurt kids if you tackle them straightforwardly. There's an example – when Gaddafi sent assassins after that high-up defector, you remember, well, they got the would-be killers. They let them think they'd done the job. Took them out to the City of the Dead and faced them with what looked like the corpse. Your real defector all right but shamming dead. They'd even got some actor in to advise on make-up. Blood, the lot. Well, that's the story and I believe it. How d'you think they got the money from the Russians to finish the High Dam then kicked them out? The point is, they really believe the fantasies they sell. Same with the *Achille Lauro* hijackers. They knew we'd intercept, a put-up job. But as far as they were concerned, they really could kid themselves and the rest of the Arab world they had clean hands.'

The car cornered sharply, throwing them together, and began to climb.

Leo wagged his head. 'Incredible.'

Charlotte said: 'I think it's brilliant, in a way.'

Something in Charlotte's tone made Leo look up and silenced Hal. Then he was calling to the driver to stop and rapping on the window. He's so sure in his skin, thought Charlotte, as if it were a good suit he put on every day. The short, evenly cut grey hair looks like a neatly mowed lawn. And along with so many powerful Americans, his face was younger than the colour of his hair. He's about fifty now but he probably looked like that at thirty.

I must be slightly drunk or very tired, she thought. Or both. Not unpleasant. A feeling of floating just above the surface of things. As Hal rolled down the window, there was that palpable scent like dust (rebuilding? demolition? desert sand?), urine-threaded, the smell of Cairo she had first been aware of at Heliopolis, where the airport had struck her as a vision of hell. Surge without direction, and stasis. No recognisable ebb or flow but burdened, weary souls, families thrust apart, calling and seeking each other across barriers.

'What's happened to Max?' she asked but no one heard her and it didn't seem to matter very much. Hal was leaning out of the car, the door open, shouting to a thin, wavering figure under the lamp.

'Niki! Will you get the hell in. Where you going?'

'Nowhere in particular. Home?'

'You're pointing in the wrong direction. Come on, we're going to the Marriott.'

'What for?'

'A few drinks.'

'Oh. Well.'

He was very thin with an interesting bony face, as if the skeleton might break through any minute. Skinny bird-neck. He slipped into the jump-seat next to Leo. He had to duck to get in and sat with his neck cricked to avoid the roof. What Charlotte noticed was his plimsolls. Not smart track shoes but good old, worn-down English plimsolls.

'Leo, Charlie, Niki. Nikolai Yussoupov when he's had a shower. The most English Russian we all know. Hobdoy Travel when he remembers.'

'Hello.'

There's something appealing about him, Charlotte was

17

thinking, and something chaotic. He's cut himself shaving. She smiled as he reached across to shake hands and then the car suddenly jolted, nearly skidded and before he could catch himself, still holding her hand, he almost fell on top of her. He could be one of those drunks, she guessed with an uncalled-for, irrelevant revelation, who show no sign until they pass out. Then the car righted itself and Hal's driver was opening the door.

Hal called after him.

'What is it, Ali?'

For a second – tiredness catching up with her, shock, something – Charlotte closed her eyes, interpreting the meaning of the impact, imagining the body. Not bleeding but some vital organ damaged. The soft thump of death. That feeling she had had as the plane slipped down the side of the world, of going into darkness.

Then she opened her eyes and the driver was back in his seat, Hal was saying: 'Nothing. Just a dog.'

'Is it hurt? Shouldn't we do something?'

'Not unless you can call up the dead.' Hal squeezed her arm. 'It was starving anyway. What a soft heart you have, Charlie.'

'No I haven't. Not at all.'

'Best hotel in Cairo,' Hal was saying as Charlotte came out of the bathroom. 'This was the old Gezira Palace. They had the ball here for the opening of the Suez Canal. You like it?'

'Wonderful,' Charlotte said.

'All phoney. But not a bad job. Keep out of the night-club but you've got to see the ballroom. Best hotel in Cairo, eh, Niki?'

'What? Oh, yes. Well. Depends what you want, I suppose.'

Nikolai was standing at the far end of the long room. Leo was refilling his glass of Scotch and carrying around the bottle. Max Stiller had disappeared but the bird-woman had joined the remains of the party that was attempting to and not quite succeeding in re-creating itself in the Hamps' suite. The Egyptian from Hal's garden had somehow caught up with them and he and Nina Fahmi – her little satin cap now slightly askew – were chattering like old friends in French. Possibly they were old friends. Masoud Suleiman was leaning to whisper something in her ear which clearly entertained her.

Charlotte wondered how soon she could decently go to bed. Leo would be no help. He was the kind of man who collects parties without ever meaning to. Something passive in his nature? She had never worked it out. As she walked past him she caught his eye and he raised his eyebrows in apology. Well, of course, everyone forgave Leo everything. Charlotte felt her wrist seized.

'Such a charming husband! You are so lucky! And so good-looking.'

'Thank you.'

Nina Fahmi was reluctant to let her go. Charlotte noticed that her purple lipstick had wandered, smudging the outline of her mouth.

'You must both come and see me in my poor home. People say Cairo is terrible but that is because they do not know it. They do not go through the door.'

'Thank you. If we can. I'm not sure there'll be time.'

Nina Fahmi released her grip to throw up her tiny hands.

'Oh! You're off on the river, I suppose, like everyone else. That boring old Nile.'

'I hope so.'

There would be more air at the far end where tall windows opened onto a balcony.

'So you're a travel agent?'

Charlotte saw that along with the plimsolls, Nikolai wore old-fashioned baggy grey flannels and a threadbare green sweater with a greasy shirt-collar showing through. He stood propped against the shutters, glass in hand, watching something going on in the garden below. The pool and the garden around were brilliantly lit. A bride, like a doll from a wedding cake, stood with her arm through the plump groom's. He was sweating and every so often a girl stepped forward and powdered his forehead. A wedding? A film of a

19

wedding? The women guests, elegantly got up in a western way, made a queer trilling noise.

'The zaghreet,' Nikolai said. 'A sort of cheer. The tongue on the roof of the mouth.' He shifted from one foot to another. One elbow stuck through a hole in his sweater. 'Hobdoy's? Yes. Not that there's much to do. It's a small firm that forgot to grow up. The big boys have pretty well taken over. Package tours, you know.'

'So what do you do?'

'Oh. This and that. You know. Whatever comes up.' He seemed, she thought, appallingly tired, she had never seen a man so tired. It was late, of course, and he probably was drunk. 'You're going on the *Hathor*? Up the river?' he asked.

Charlotte had thought of it as down, something to do with the sun, as if you could get on at Cairo and slide right down Africa into the sun. But of course, it was up. The source lay beyond reach except by plane, something to be imagined beyond the starving and the troubles and the deserts: she saw a tropical zone, a bright spring rising.

'That's the idea.'

'You'll enjoy that.'

A shot rang out and the noise of the dying party was cut off for a moment as below, by the pool, a robed Arab figure strode towards the tented dais where bride and groom stood eternally smiling. The intruder pulled a pistol from his robes and fired. The director was apparently not satisfied, the assassin retreated and fired again. And again.

It was a knife not a gun in Phoebe's house, Charlotte reflected as she tried to sleep. Did death come from within her own household or from the desert, through that other Egyptian garden? Would she find the missing passages of the journal in Luxor? Aswan? Perhaps they had never been written, or written and seized and scattered by the holder of the knife or destroyed by a discreet servant protecting the reputation of the Sayyida.

Charlotte had had the idea of coming on this trip and by the way excavating a dead truth. The truth about a death.

But lying in the big bed in the beautiful suite, her face against Leo's warm, golden shoulder, she had an intimation like a shadow that this was a place of illusions and secrets, façades and silences, a country in which she might find what she was looking for and could be utterly lost.

2

'Allah Akbar!'

What? Awake? Where? Only just gone to sleep. Leo offering coffee. Light? Was that daylight?

'Ashhado an la illa Allah!'

'Feeling better?' Leo kissed her, eased up a pillow behind her. Charlotte took the cup of coffee. For a second she could not remember where she was. A darkness. Then Leo flung open the shutters, drew the curtains and opened a window. The cry that had been a faint thread in her dream was now shrilly commanding, even above the racket of the city. Leo stood in an oblong of brilliant light, exactly where whatsisname had stood last night. Nikolai.

Charlotte swallowed her coffee. At Leo's shoulder she looked down and saw the scene of last night's film. It might have been a dream: all signs that it had ever happened had vanished. Already someone was swimming in the pool, sprinklers were turning on the grass, the gravel was being raked. She took a deep breath: sun, a wonderful dry heat, light.

'Better?'

Leo put an arm round her. She turned her head to look at him. Years and years you can have with someone, then one day you raise your head and catch an unguarded expression and you think: I don't really know him at all.

'Well, you were a bit prickly last night.'

'Was I? Oh, you mean Hal. I just get bored with Hal. You know – the thing about the Egyptians is.' The sound of a pneumatic drill or a pile-driver, muffled by the garden.

'Hal's all right.'

'Oh yes.' Charlotte shrugged. 'It's just that I feel. The

22

American Centre. You know. He's never really left home. I expect we were the same when we had an empire.'

She thought of the pages she had read on the plane, Phoebe's early journal notes, scribbled quickly, the writing dashing and untidy with excitement. She saw her writing those words that were so different from the letters or the later journal, never meant to be read. Lying with her new husband in the hotel at Aswan, the fan creaking as it turned, the beautiful gardens, the pink granite falling away down to the Nile. Love at the edge of the tropics inside the bridal fall of the mosquito net. The gargle of soft brown doves. The trees that seemed to be in white bloom or full of butterflies. 'Alex says they are egrets. Just as he spoke they all took flight, leaving the tree bereft.'

Bereft. Bereaved. Beautiful words.

Wasn't there a bird called a mourning dove?

Leo was saying: 'You missed some fun going to bed.'

'How long did it go on?'

'About two, three o'clock. Niki disappeared and we found he'd gone to sleep in the bath.'

'What did you do? Is he still there?'

'God, no. He'd passed out cold. Hal wasn't having him in his swanky limo so we heaved him downstairs and into a cab. Hal paid. The driver knew where to take him. They all do. He's a regular customer at that time of night. Usually at someone else's expense. Well, you ready to do the tourist bit? Hal's people have laid on a mini-bus for ten o'clock. Saqqara and Giza. Memphis optional.'

'You're not coming?'

Leo kissed her cheek. Charlotte watched a sparrow picking among invisible crumbs on the balcony.

'Wish I could. I'll go alone later. Maybe tomorrow. Anyhow, got to check out some hotels, if they're still there. As you may have noticed, Cairo's falling down.'

The little bird looked at them, its head tipped sideways. Even in the cool of the room Charlotte could feel the heat building. A hot breath. Behind her Leo was dressing.

23

'Who was that girl with Nina Fahmi last night? The one in the brown kaftan?'

'Who? Oh, that's Adila. Nina's niece by marriage. Her father's a rich dentist, I think. Just another of Hal's crowd.'

'She's rather beautiful.'

'Is she? I suppose she is. You'd better get on or you'll miss the bus. The others have done the Egyptian museum already.'

In the shower Charlotte let the water run through her crinkly fair hair. The same as her great-aunt's, so far as she could judge from one of the few pictures of Phoebe.

She called to Leo: 'Is Nikolai really a travel agent?'

'Hardly know him. On and off, I think. He's a bit deceptive. Spends his day topping up his alcohol level and stone cold sober at crack of dawn, Hal says.'

Charlotte stepped out of the shower and reached for a towel. Her eyes were shut against the soap when she felt Leo's arms round her.

She laughed and kissed him back blindly.

'You'll get soaked. Give me the towel!'

The golden head between her breasts. Then gently he wiped her eyes, first one, then the other, then he kissed them.

'I don't want to go.'

'I don't want you to go. Your suit's soaking.'

'It'll dry on me in five minutes in this heat. Sorry about last night,' he said. 'Lost count of the time.'

'No, you're not. You enjoyed every minute.'

'And you didn't mind too much?' His expression was anxious.

'I didn't mind at all.'

'See you later then. You ready?'

Ready? she wondered. Leo had gone. Charlotte was alone in the room. There had been no time to unpack and she took the first cotton dress she found in the suitcase. No need to lock. (The thing about the Egyptians, Hal said, is they never steal.) Her fingers touched the thick file at the bottom of the

24

case but she resisted the temptation to pull it out. Ancient history, she thought. Why bother? Letters from the dead.

Hurry, they'll be waiting. Blue dress. Sandals. No, Hal had said canvas shoes (the thing about the Egyptians is they shit in the sand). Scarf? Yes. Light woven shoulder-bag, ethnic, Leo's present from Syria, years ago, he had one the same. Sun-cream. Sunglasses. She saw Phoebe waiting, packed away for the moment in shadows, layers of darkness. She closed the shutters against the heat, paused for a moment by the bed. She could see their shapes, hers and Leo's; she had left hardly a mark but where his big body had lain the sheet was tangled, a pillow thrown off and the other pillow still hollowed where his head had pressed. Imprints.

Charlotte touched his pillow, tracing the shape of his head. Then she went downstairs, out, into the sun.

Max Stiller rode a camel. That is, wearing a white sun-hat with a green lining, he allowed himself bravely to be led the few hundred yards up the street to the Pyramid of Cheops. His legs did not reach the clumsy stirrups.

Afterwards, sitting by Charlotte in the mini-bus, he mopped his forehead.

'Exhausting pleasures. The touts have taken over.' His glance was shrewd. 'You were disappointed?'

Charlotte wondered. 'Saqqara was marvellous. The desert. You can touch the silence. But this.' She felt odd, dizzy. Phoebe had had the same thin skin, colouring. What had she said about the heat? 'But here, the guide, all that talk, the crowds. I couldn't see. It was better last night. I kept thinking, if I could be alone. It was exactly as I had imagined and yet it was less than I imagined. D'you know what I mean?'

They had had a snack at the Mena House and were bumping back into town.

Max nodded. 'Yes, it's too much to take in. Flaubert's my man.'

After all, they were not going to Memphis. Egypt had changed her mind. The streets narrowed. Charlotte saw

25

something like a country village challenging the city: hens, skinny dogs, goats grazing on a rubbish heap, children running beside the bus, grinning, thumping on the windows.

'Flaubert?'

'His journal and letters. While Maxime du Camp was measuring a temple Flaubert saw a yellow cow put her head round the corner. He said that was what mattered: the yellow cow.'

Charlotte laughed.

'But you've had to do years of research. For Joseph.'

'That is why I have come again,' Max said. 'I am looking for the yellow cow.'

Charlotte smiled, did not say because she could not explain in terms that might be interesting the horror she had felt entering, first descending, then climbing the passages into the centre of the great Pyramid. Claustrophobia, of course, airlessness, the press of bodies behind and before. Weird acoustics, whispering walls. And then, where she had expected if not a revelation at least an intimation (a reward), in that central chamber there was the horror of nothing. Empty sarcophagus. The impulse to curl into a foetus, cover one's ears against the blank voice of eternity.

And now she was looking down into the crypt of St Sergius. An elderly American-sounding couple she had noticed on the mini-bus were using flash cameras. The effect was of lightning. After each flash the shabby little place seemed darker. The guide was informing them that this was the area of the Coptic churches. In this crypt Mary and Joseph with the child Jesus had hidden in their flight from Herod into Egypt. ('Not your Joseph,' Charlotte smiled at Max, who wagged his head. He seemed pale and there were beads of sweat on his brow.)

'Wouldn't you like to sit down? Go back to the coach?' Charlotte suggested.

Max's reply was almost impatient.

'No, no. I must pay my respects to Ben Ezra.'

He trotted beside her through ever-narrowing streets that

became hardly more than passages. The narrowing was not alarming like the tunnel into the Great Pyramid. There was filth and a strong smell of dung, animal, possibly human. Life, anyway. Behind a grille a woman's laughter. Men gossiping, children, a child clutching a one-eared cat to her chest like a doll. Then a shady garden.

'A synagogue in the land of our foes,' Max said wryly. 'They were even rebuilding though you would never believe it.'

'But however . . .?'

'The Jews bought it from the Copts. Here the Romans destroyed the temple of Jeremiah. Here may have been Babylon. But these stories. There are too many stories in Egypt. Here however I may seek out the rabbi and whisper shalom.'

'I think I'll wait outside.'

It was wonderful how the banyan tree fingered the earth, probed for life in the poor soil, renewed itself. There was something sagacious about it. After the sad Coptic churches with their dust and their relics, their sense of lost, despairing voices, a mumble of confused faiths and tongues and prayers, this calm Indian tree held the possibility of eternity.

'Missis, missis!'

Charlotte opened her eyes. One of those Arab youths who were everywhere in this quarter of the city, shadows one minute, eager, nervously snatching substance the next, was pulling at her sleeve.

'Missis! Your father sick! Very bad!'

'I have no father.'

It was Max, stumbling out of the synagogue, waving away hands that would help. Charlotte jumped to her feet.

'Nothing,' he said. 'It is nothing.'

The mini-bus had come to join them.

'You must sit down. What happened?'

'A stupid fuss. A little turn in there, that was all.'

'Let me call a taxi.'

But he insisted, no. In the bus he closed his eyes. Only back at the hotel did he allow Charlotte to accompany him at least to the door of his room. No doctor, he said. In the air-conditioned cool he was breathing better. A small sheikh in robes so long he might have been on castors came past leading his veiled and twittering harem.

'You'll call me if you need anything?'

'That is very kind. It will not be necessary. You have been very kind.'

In her own room Charlotte showered, thought of ordering tea, then saw the roses. Surely the wrong season for roses, even in Egypt. Someone had put them in water. Waxy white, they shone in the dim room as if they had been sprayed. She touched a petal.

Odd, she thought, no card. She glanced through the other messages. Mostly for Leo. One from Leo, reminding her to be ready by seven. What for? She could not remember.

She looked at the telephone. No, if Max were asleep what would be the point in waking him?

On an impulse she pulled out the thick file from the suitcase. She slipped between the cool sheets, opened the file and took out a page at random.

Cairo, January 1919

Dearest Dorothy,

Mother will be getting my note from Suez, I hope, and will share it with you. So by the time you read this you will know that P. & O. delivered me safely and we were not blown up by lurking mines. Also that the Red Sea is not red but the most astonishing blue. And my darling Alex came straight on board to carry me off to our delayed honeymoon. One day I can tell you all about our voyage upriver and our happiness at Aswan, and I can say now that while I'm glad enough to have the life here for a while (very busy! and I'm grateful you bullied me into all those ridiculous party frocks!), I long to go home. That is, Aswan. My taste for that place is regarded

as very eccentric. I think I have already broken the rules
in liking it, and the English matrons of Cairo *want* to be sorry
for me that I have to make my life there.

Meanwhile, Cairo is fun. Alex went off this morning to
the Gezira Sporting Club and there is to be a fancy dress ball
at Shepheard's. But what I want to do most – and this is *not*
for Mother's ears or eyes – is to know the Egyptians better.
Or rather, to find out who the Egyptians are, they are such a
muddle – Copts and Turks and French and Armenians . . .
but please tell Mother that we have taken on one good servant
called Amir. I liked him at once, he had good recommendations
and I truly believe him to be trustworthy.

Here is Alex back. Write soon. That's all I lack, news
of you and M. and everyone.

And now I am to tell Amir who will tell the cook (who
is his wife or his sister or his sister-in-law, I don't know) what
to serve for dinner. Imagine me – a housewife!

With all my love and a (brotherly) salute from Alex —
Phoebe

While Charlotte slept at last, abruptly, deeply, Max Stiller lay
on his bed waiting for the pill to work. Meanwhile the cold
flannel on his forehead helped and the other tricks he had
learned. Loosen the trousers, of course. Breathe lightly like
a woman in labour, coasting the pain. Hot-water bottle? No.
Too much effort to lift the telephone, explain.

Ah. Easier. An old fool he'd been to go on the trip today.
To come to Egypt at all.

Yes, definitely better. Still, move slowly. Spectacles. Sleep
would be best but first, book. Where was it? Ah, there it is
on the bedside table. Budge. Tell me a story. The one I
know by heart.

> I shall live, I shall live; I shall germinate, I shall germinate, I
> shall germinate; I shall wake up in peace; I shall not putrefy;
> my intestines shall not perish; I shall not suffer injury.

The vital organs were preserved in canopic jars. Take them,
Anubis, any time you like. What's left of them.

Beautiful though, Max thought: the ancients' goodnight story for those afraid of the weighing of the soul, the judgment of Osiris.

His spectacles slipped from his nose, the book from his hand. He slept.

'Well, it's not really Hal's bash, of course,' Leo said, holding on to the strap as the taxi, a part of Cairo's permanent traffic jam, saw a space ahead on the El Gala bridge and flung itself forward. The driver seemed remarkably equable. There was something cheerful about the chaos, as if this were a social occasion. The cacophony of horns might have been greeting each other. Every so often a pedestrian strode casually through, patting a bonnet, grinning and calling and miraculously, it seemed to Charlotte, reaching the other side.

Charlotte said: 'I haven't seen the Nile yet, properly. What d'you mean?' A sheen there, of oil on water?

Leo grinned. 'Well, so far as I can gather. Or, rather, my guess is, tourism's falling off badly. There's been that hijacking, the Fundamentalist riots and a bit of bumping-off of the odd diplomat and tripper. Mostly American, British and Israeli. A nasty little would-be colonels' junta. A news blackout. Rumours, half of them true. Enough to keep the visitors away. Last time the Americans and the Japanese cancelled en bloc.'

'But what's that got to do with Hal?'

'The Egyptians want to convince us that this is a stable country. So Hal puts up the idea. He lets the Egyptians use the name of the Centre for respectability, they don't look too closely at the guest-list and pay up. Probably from American subsidies and certainly a little on top for Hal. The sort of arrangement that would appeal to both parties.'

'How on earth do you know this?'

'I don't. I know Hal. Oh, and that Suleiman chap is doing a freelance job for the Ministry.'

'Extraordinary.'

They had turned left now, released at last from the bridge

into another stream of traffic. Vaguely, Charlotte could make out house-boats moored to the bank.

'It's hard to imagine. Terrorism, all that,' Charlotte said. 'The Egyptians seem so friendly.'

'So they are. The Cairenes you are likely to meet, anyway. They will say that they have always loved the British and we are supposed to believe them. Mustn't spoil the party. By the way, how's the Phoebe stuff getting on?'

'It's not, so far. I haven't got down to it.'

(I truly believe, Mother, that Amir would give his life for us – all of us but especially for the children. Since Robin and Pansy were born . . .)

'What's that?'

'The Zoological Gardens. This way for the animals.'

Here, on the opposite side of the road from the Zoo, the houses were, or had once been, imposing. An architecture Charlotte thought of vaguely as colonial. Much of it shabby, as if a dusty hand had been wiped across its face, the lights put out, the gardens left suddenly to a cruder nature that flourished even here in the heart of the city. The one they were making for was blanked off from the road by high walls. Leo paid off the cab, offered his arm for Charlotte to take and under the street lamp said: 'You look stunning. Up the aisle then?'

An armed guard yawned in a sentry-box at the tall iron gates, made a sketch of standing straight and, with his cigarette held behind his back, inspected their invitations, nodded and called to the gate-man.

As they walked through the long garden towards the house, Charlotte squeezed Leo's hand. So many seasons a marriage has. What if the Adila girl had fallen for him? What if he had responded? Leo was the only man she knew who truly loved women. There was a kind of innocence about his philandering (if he did philander), a passionate curiosity as if, being born, he had woken up in a field of wonderful flowers. Charlotte smiled wryly to herself at the picture of Leo bounding with goodwill and enquiry from a rose to a lily to a tulip.

31

'You'd always come back to me, wouldn't you?' she said as they climbed the steps to the house.

And then before he could answer she said: 'I think Egypt's good for us.'

Then she remembered she had forgotten to thank him for the roses.

'I'm afraid we missed the Serapeum.'

Nina Fahmi shuddered.

'A perfectly awful place! I thought I would quite lose my mind there. Sarcophagi for dead bulls! *J'avais une telle migraine!*'

The little woman touched her forehead with one perfectly manicured finger, recalling and indicating perhaps the precise location of the pain in her head.

'The best thing to be said about it is that it stopped. Apparently quite suddenly. I tell you, my dear, those ancients there is such a fuss about were nothing but *barbares*. All noise and superstition and bombast and corruption. How else were they overrun? So frequently? And I suppose you will go on that frightful river and get a bend in the neck looking up at their ridiculous temples.'

'I'm looking forward to the river. I've hardly seen it yet,' Charlotte said. The room was large and high-ceilinged, reserved, Charlotte guessed, for official functions. Red flocked wallpaper, smeared in places as though a lizard had slithered down it, a chandelier that might once have been splendid, unused, and in its place the usual dim lighting. Enough though to give back the reflection of the party from the floor-to-ceiling mirrors, framed in time-crazed gilt. So that, in the corner where she stood, not one but three Nina Fahmis – tonight in a turban of black silk shot with gold – raised her small hands in the characteristic clutching gesture of horror. She looked like a bird about to perch. Then in mid-shriek pounced. She took a glass from a passing waiter and dipped her beak.

'Never, never, ever, I beg you, put in so much as one little toe!'

32

'Is it so dirty?'

'Well, obviously, a drain! But I am talking about the bilharzia worm which will enter even through one toe and destroy your liver.'

'How awful.'

'What is so awful?' Today the girl, Adila, was in Western dress. Simple black wool, expensive, Charlotte judged. Her long brown hair caught back in a gold band, no make-up. Charlotte felt overdressed, gross, white, gingery. 'Auntie, you must not tell Mrs Hamp bad stories about Egypt.'

'Adila!' Nina presented her cheek to be kissed.

'You see, Mrs Hamp,' Adila said, 'my aunt is not Egyptian. Masoud, help me.' Suleiman had joined them. He bowed his head to Charlotte and kissed Nina. Charlotte remembered what Max had said about him, her own first impression, the sight of him in the suite at the Marriott whispering secrets to Nina.

But this was a different Suleiman. He had put on with a sober dark suit some gravity, an air of officialdom. Of course. Leo had said he had been coopted by the Ministry. He wore a tag in his lapel announcing his office.

Charlotte smiled.

'I gather you are one of our hosts.'

'Only in Cairo, Mrs Hamp.'

Adila was drinking orange juice. She said: 'Masoud, Auntie's been telling Mrs Hamp that Egypt is dirty and poor and disgusting.'

'No, really — ' Charlotte was embarrassed.

Masoud's tone was solemn.

'There is no poverty in Egypt, Mrs Hamp. You will see for yourself on the river. The fellahin are well-fed and happy. There is compulsory education over the age of twelve years. Our industry is developing. We are drilling for water in the desert. Cairo has become a world centre for expositions. We have shows of weapons systems, book fairs.'

'Oh, I'm sure,' Charlotte said and at the same time had the feeling that this was yet another piece of theatre. It would be discourteous to argue or to question. Yet at the back of his eyes was he laughing? At her? With her? She sensed a deep irony.

Nina clucked.

'You are no fun tonight, Masoud. And you, Adila, are quite absurd. I ask you, Mrs Hamp, you tell me why when my pretty niece here could do nothing at all but think of ways to enjoy herself, instead she goes to the Sorbonne. And then, when she could stay in Paris forever, she comes back here to become of all things a tourist guide! Four years of qualifying herself to become a dragoman!'

'It used to be an honourable profession, Auntie.'

'And in Cairo there are honourable whores. Now, where is your beautiful husband, Mrs Hamp?'

'Please. My name is Charlotte.'

'Very good. Charming. Charlotte. Then let us find dear Hal who will rescue us from all these stiff-wigs and take us to a night-club. Where you may see bad belly-dancing.'

At the far end of the room a speech was made into a microphone on the blink. There was polite applause. Not enough drink: as the speech-making began the waiters withdrew. The Minister of Tourism welcomed the distinguished guests. On the wall behind him hung the flags of Egypt, the United States, France, Britain, Germany, Italy, Japan. The Union flag was upside down. The microphone squealed and another speaker was saying something about the new metro system, irrigation, new cities, and farms that would make the desert bloom again; the weaving workshops subsidised by the government in the countryside around Cairo one of which tomorrow they would have the opportunity of visiting and where the children of the rural workers were instructed in traditional skills.

A less enthusiastic tribute was paid to the cooperation of the American Centre. There were more words. The antiquities of the most ancient civilisation on earth. The gift of the river. The experience of the Nile for those who were continuing their visit to our country on the *Hathor*. But at

34

the same time not to be overlooked by the friends of Egypt gathered here, her place as natural leader of the Arab world, a force for peace, progress and stability to which those from East and West might turn with confidence.

'And they invented the biro,' said Hal, taking Charlotte's elbow. 'Come on, let's get out of here.'

The speeches were over. Charlotte looked for Leo, saw the elderly American – or it might be Canadian – couple from the Coptic church (the woman waved), and accepted, along with everyone leaving the room, the glossy hand-out booklet with a photograph of Ramses II on the front, the heavy-featured President on the back. Both faces unreadable. Oddly, of the two, the dead Pharaoh with his smile of power, self-congratulation, seemed both more alarming and more alive.

'A real Arab place,' Hal said as his black limousine swept them along like a magic carriage, by the Nile, through the now nearly empty road. One of the house-boats was decorated with fairy-lights. The colours shook as though in some other element and then Charlotte noticed a dash of rain against the black window through which they could see but not be seen.

'It's raining!'

'It's March, Charlie. Winter. You thought it never rained in Egypt?'

'Well. I suppose it must. It is.'

'Two different climates. Cairo and the South.'

Charlotte remembered the hoar-frost morning at Heathrow, when, watching the planes take off, waiting to check in, she had glanced idly through Phoebe's journal and imagined the place of dry sun and white sky. It would still be there. Meanwhile, for this evening, she felt suspended between the reality of a shower in Cairo and the vision she could not yet fully grasp of that other world, south.

Hal wound down the window and spoke to the chauffeur.

'Sharia Alfi. The Cleopatra.'

Just as they were about to turn off the main road to cross back over another bridge to Zamalek, the chauffeur braked

35

abruptly and a military-looking vehicle overtook and passed them. The driver yelled to the chauffeur who returned the insult or greeting in Arabic. In the back of the truck Charlotte caught a glimpse of boys in ill-fitting khaki, hanging on to the frame to keep their balance, the oily glint of weapons. They handled the rifles like toys, waving them at the big, black car. Playing or threatening, it was hard to tell.

Leo blinked. He should wear glasses and did not: a vanity that sometimes amused, sometimes irritated Charlotte.

'What's that all about?' he asked Hal.

'Usual nerves. Edgier than usual maybe.'

'The Fundamentalists?'

'Not just them. The colonel's gang and the New Wafd wanting democracy. Well, what do you do? The population will be sixty-five million by the middle of the next decade. Housing problems, water-supply problems. The Arab League problem. The Israeli problem. Your Egyptian character. Democracy Shemocracy. They wouldn't know how to deal with it. What they want is Nasser back. What's the joke, Charlie?'

'I have just been told there is no poverty in Egypt. Officially.'

Hal snorted.

'Without the US they'd be living in cardboard boxes. Hey, Ali, where you going? First to the right, not the left. Fucking natives.'

Charlotte drew in her breath but the driver turned his head, showing a beaming black face.

Under the tented ceiling, before the low ottomans arranged in a semi-circle, the noise first struck Charlotte as appalling. They had arrived late when the show had already started and, meaning to drink no more, she had absently accepted Hal's refills, hardly aware even that it was whisky she was drinking. There seemed to be nothing to eat but the dips arranged before them on the low tables. Hal, beside her, said: 'Ah! this is good, you are seeing the real thing!' Charlotte looked for

36

Leo and saw he was on the opposite side of the semi-circle between Masoud and Adila. Nina and her niece appeared to be the only women there who were not foreigners.

Leo laughed, throwing back his head, at something Masoud had said. Charlotte wondered what the joke was (was she jealous? Of Adila? Of Leo's capacity for enjoying himself, always, anywhere?). Her mind wandered, the music seemed shrill, cacophonous. Two young men were prancing, dancing, grinning, leaping as though on hot coals. A wailing song, cries, then whatever story they were telling was done. As the belly dancer came on – commanding – Charlotte heard something in the music she had not expected. The deep-throated voice of Africa. A solemn, then urgent, then frenzied drumbeat.

She was caught up. It was not the belly but the arms, the most minute shuddering movement of one hip, and then at the climax at the centre of the dance, a stillness so purely sensual it transcended sensuality.

Charlotte realised she had been holding her breath when the spell was ended, and the dancer released her audience. Then flowers were thrown on stage, there were whistles, applause, a frenzy of adoration.

'The most famous whore in Cairo, of course,' said Nina Fahmi. 'My husband would never allow me to go to such places. But Adila's generation . . . what can one do?'

Charlotte made an effort to smile. From the night-club Hal had carried them off on a tour of his drinking holes. It struck Charlotte with the surprise of small revelations, that he was a lonely man. Even now, in the deep sofas of the Marriott lounge, he was trying to keep the party going. He wanted to wake up Max, call Niki.

Even Leo groaned no. Yet no one seemed inclined to part, as if their being together were some kind of safety, reassurance against darkness. Outside the rain fell more heavily. A package tour was herded in and stood blinking with exhaustion, stunned.

Charlotte said to Nina: 'Were you here in the 1920s?'

'Oh yes, I have been here forever. Too long among these

37

Egyptians.' Nina remembered herself. 'Naturally, I was very young. A child bride.'

'I wondered if you ever met an English couple. Phoebe and Alex Duncan? She came out to be married about then.'

'The name is familiar but there were so many names.' A flicker in Nina's expression and then some decision taken. She knew something, Charlotte was convinced, but she was choosing not to remember. It was too late, everyone was too tired, this was not the time. Or it was Nina's whim not to remember. 'There were so many secrets in those days, there still are. These Egyptians! Look at Masoud there, cooking up some secret with your beautiful husband.' For a second Charlotte thought she had gone to sleep. Then the old woman's bright little eyes snapped open again. 'I will tell you something about that time. These children, the Egyptians, put their secrets in a box. You have heard of the Bocca del Leone in Venice? The Lion's Mouth? Well, this was the same. On the wall outside the governorate. Into this box, as though they were confiding in Allah himself, they slipped their horrid little notes. Their fears and their spites. The mysteries they had woven themselves that frightened them. Denunciations. Petitions. I caught my own maid. I slapped her and she confessed she had put a hex upon her sister-in-law that her sons might die! But it was not Allah who read their dirty letters. It was the Special Secrets Clerk.'

Nina sighed. 'Now I am tired. I shall go home. But when you think the Egyptians are so charming, such a simple, happy people, remember the Bocca.'

The package tour was ostentatiously ignored by the reception clerks in their striped waistcoats and stiff collars. Even their own waiter stood over Hal, fretting for the bill to be signed, clicking his fingers.

'OK, OK,' said Hal. He stood. ''Night, Charlie. Leo, Sol. Adila, you are so bloody beautiful. Come on, Nina, drop you off.'

At the last moment of parting, Nina, suddenly quite sober, wide-awake, kissed Charlotte's cheek.

'Don't look too deep, my dear. Sometimes it is better not to look.'

'I forgot to say,' Charlotte said, 'thank you for the roses.'

But Leo was already asleep.

Charlotte lay awake. She had passed the point of tiredness. The whisky had tasted sour.

Guiltily, she remembered Max but it was too late to check if he was all right. As he got into bed Leo had said something about Masoud and Adila tomorrow.

She heard the rain on the window and slipping at last into sleep, thought of the box on the wall and all those small, sad secrets and the people who had come by night to put them there, as if by so doing, they could shake off past terrors, present fears.

3

'My husband. I cannot find my husband.'

They had seemed disinclined to notice Charlotte at the reception desk. They looked like well-groomed starlings and had an air of extreme busyness without actually doing anything. She felt invisible and when finally she caught the attention of one of the starlings, faintly foolish. Well, it had been absurd to worry. She had woken to find Leo not there.

'Your room number, Madame?'

'315.'

'The key of 315 has not been left.'

'Well, of course not. I have it. I am looking for Mr Hamp. Mr Leo Hamp.'

'He will be in the coffee-shop, perhaps.'

'He's not in the coffee-shop.'

The sketch of a shrug. There are husbands. Husbands may be lost. It is possible this woman is mad. She never had a husband and so he is not lost.

The starling brightened. Not for Charlotte's benefit. A large man who smelled expensive and wore a suit with the sheen of silk, like fitted upholstery, was handing in his key.

'Thank you, sir. Have a nice day.'

Charlotte insisted.

'Will you see, please, if there is a message for Mrs Hamp, 315.'

'You will have to ask the message clerk.'

'The message clerk is not there.'

Almost, he turned his back on her. Then, with the weariness of one who knows that never in this life will he be adequately tipped, Charlotte's clerk walked a few steps, grumbled in Arabic to a colleague and, with deliberate slowness, returned holding a folded piece of paper.

'Missis L. Hamp?'

'Yes.'

Gone to Giza with Masoud. See you later. Love, L.

'Good morning.'

'Dr Stiller. I'm sorry. You made me jump.' Charlotte was still holding the slip of paper.

'I hope you do not have bad news?' Max handed in his key.

'Oh no. Leo's gone to the Pyramids. He missed yesterday.'

'Ah yes. They are making more discoveries. You said your husband was interested in archaeology. Perhaps he has persuaded someone to take him where the tourist cannot go.'

'Masoud. He says he's gone with Masoud.'

Max nodded. 'As I said, the fixer. Masoud will have fixed it.'

Charlotte remembered. 'Are you better? Were you all right last night? I meant to ask but we got back late.'

'Oh yes, thank you. Entirely. Are you going out?'

'Not just yet, I think. You?'

'The museum. There is a theory – not new, but lately a popular one – that the mummy of Yuya, the grand vizier, may be none other than the Biblical Yu-Seph. The implications would be extraordinary, since Yuya married into the Pharaonic dynasty. He could have been the grandfather of Akhenaton.'

'But if they're right – your research? Your book?'

Max smiled wryly.

'I might have to put it away. Or rewrite. In return I may look upon the face of Joseph today. A recompense.'

Max raised the white sun-hat with the green lining and Charlotte smiled as she watched the little man cross the foyer.

*

There must be a discrepancy somewhere between the journals and letters that would hold a clue. Yet whenever she tried to concentrate, even to get the papers in order, Charlotte found herself absorbed, utterly distracted, by the immediacies of Phoebe's writings.

Cairo, April 1919

Mother, you must not fuss on my account. I am sure the reports of the disturbances have been exaggerated in the English papers. General Bulfin cracked down and everything was normal by the end of March in this part of the country. All that saddens me is that they had to send a special expedition to Aswan this month but that will be settled too, I know. Alex says the Turks and the Germans had been plotting since before the war started. Zaghlul Pasha was the ring-leader and it was his exile that sparked the whole thing off.

But what you cannot understand at home is the true, solid underlying relationship between the Egyptians and the British. At least, they seem to me such a dignified, courteous people – I have met nothing but friendliness everywhere. There was no sign of the troubles to come when we were in Aswan – where I have left my heart.

Alex is very optimistic about the appointment of General Allenby as High Commissioner. He served under him, as you know, and says he is a man of reason and moderation who understands the Arabs.

I must stop for a moment. A Mrs Forbes from the Residency has sent in her card to call so I must be the respectable English junior bride (when I would so much rather ride with Alex in the desert or write to you).

. . . She has gone! And that was the most boring half hour I have spent since I got here. All gossip and grumbles about servants as if we were in Sevenoaks. I must tell you now before I burst that Alex has not been idle since he resigned his commission. I think he would have worked as a file-clerk just to stay on here. But it looks as if he might get a political job. Meanwhile, I have been to the Bazaar (Amir trotting behind me, don't worry!) and am sending some wonderful Syrian silk for your birthday . . . I cannot tell you how happy I am here.

Just written to Mother. Played down the March situation.
Not that I was ever in any danger – we're so insulated.
Am beginning to kick against that now things have quietened
down. Told the truth about the basic Egyptian-British relationship. That is, when the Englishman is someone like Alex
or Allenby, who both respect the Arabs.

I loathe and despise most of the Residency crowd – polo
and bridge and parties. Alex promises I shall meet some
'real' Egyptians soon. This country so brilliant, beautiful,
different from anything I've ever seen. Do so want to
know it . . . Picnic in the desert. All wonderful. A.
says I'm the best horsewoman he has ever married.
Must learn Arabic. Get recipe for Baba-ghanoug. Egg-
plant? Here everything coming into bloom – orange-trees,
palms, oleanders.

Charlotte flicked through the pages haphazardly. Nayra. A
name that came up increasingly. And Ahmed. Much later, a
birth. Notes about diet for children. One line near the end,
1924, the writing changing, spikier, thinner, as if Phoebe
were running out of ink or using a twisted nib.

It is as though there were a shadow . . . but I shall trust.
Trust whom? Why in the course of the enquiry had no one
been traced who could throw any light on the tragedy? It
was as though, that terrible day on Elephantine Island,
perpetrators, witnesses, anyone who might have had an
opinion, anyone who cared: all had vanished or refused to
speak. Or been silenced?

When Charlotte had found the box of papers in the attic,
her mother said: take them, they're your sort of thing.
It seemed to have nothing to do with the family, as far
as Ethne was concerned. Charlotte's mother, the widow,
buried her husband, lost weight, learned to drive, played
fiendish bridge, gave her garden the patience she had never
shown for anyone, anything. Storing the dahlia corms,
planning for the spring, ordering bulbs from Lincolnshire by
mail-order. She disapproved of Charlotte, considered her

grief excessive; she had never trained Charlotte for grief or joy. In consequence Charlotte, like a princess cursed by a wicked fairy, never learned to cry. And Howard, who might have had passion in him once, retreated to his workshop or his study where he studied nothing anyone was aware of. Ethne would cope, she always did. If she had told him on his death-bed to climb into his coffin so that she could change the sheets, he would have done so.

Ethne had said: well, of course, she was on your father's side of the family – Phoebe.

Ethne did say once, clearing up, chucking out Howard's life, offering Charlotte a soap-stone Nefertiti: your father always wanted to go to Egypt. As she might say: to the zoo.

August, 1919

Ahmed tells me that to become a Moslem all one has to
do is to say 'There is no God but Allah. Mohammed is
the Prophet of Allah.' Tempted to say it there and then but
though I believe Nayra and Ahmed are real friends (not
the Mrs Forbes sort), that might give offence. All the same,
said it quietly to myself when I was alone. Felt no different!
Am determined to go to the Khan el Khalili bazaar without
a bodyguard. I mean, with Nayra perhaps. Copper wonderful
and ivory but scent of spices best . . . All the wives
talk about going to Alexandria to get away from the heat.
Told Alex, I won't go. Is he cross?

Charlotte was not at all sure how she had reached this part of the city. Except that after the chambermaid's third knock and retreat, she had locked away the journals and letters (how absurd, whoever would want to steal them?), and left the hotel.

She refused the doorman's offer of a cab and walked vaguely in the direction they had driven last night, across one of the bridges. The Sheraton blocked the way she was looking for, down to the Nile, so she walked through the foyer and out onto the terrace. A wind she had not been aware of whipped up the river, flinging spray in her face and on the loungers and the tables. The parasols were furled and folded, waiters absent, and there was something oppressive, desolate about the place in spite of its brave flags. These hotels were like latterday temples or fortresses that might any night be emptied of such life as they had. Charlotte had a vision of them as pock-marked ruins.

She looked at her map. Dokki. She liked the sound of that. And so plunged into the narrower streets, away from the frantic main road, was lost again but did not mind too much. Then came suddenly, just as she felt she could walk no further, upon this quiet square of dusty palms and balding grass.

Sitting thankfully on the bench, Charlotte saw boys kicking a football around under the trees, another resting against a palm, apparently asleep in the deepest shade, then waking to shout at the players, something mocking. A skinny dog played with the boys and the boys and the dog and the sleeper made a dance, a pattern, that was somehow beautiful. There was a public building. A woman hanging out washing on a roof, calling to someone indoors. A goat tethered on the roof. Posher flats. Someone practising clumsy scales on a piano. Signals from secret lives. For the first time Charlotte had a pleasing intimation of this chaotic, dirty, sprawling city as not so alien after all: a place one could, with patience, begin to grasp. Phoebe had been impatient. There was an escapade with her friend, Nayra, the plan, confided to her journal, to dress in the very habit Nayra despised. The veil of invisibility, Phoebe called it.

'Bon?'

'I'm sorry, I don't understand.'

Charlotte had nearly dozed off. She smiled at the girl in the grubby kaftan.

'German? America?'

'No. British. English.'

'Good! English. Bon? Café? Café turc?'

The girl pointed in the direction of gardens at the end

45

of the square. There, presumably, she brewed whatever it was she was offering.

Charlotte shook her head. The girl smiled back but her attentions had brought others: children holding out their hands. The boys had noticed. The football arced through the air and just as it might have landed in Charlotte's lap, Niki Yussoupov caught it and kicked it back.

'La shukran,' he said and the girl and the children ran off giggling. He shouted something in Arabic to the boys and they laughed and resumed their game.

'Thanks,' Charlotte said. 'I was a bit stuck there.'

He stood over her, hands in pockets. The same thread-bare sweater and plimsolls.

'They wouldn't have hurt you.'

Looking up, she couldn't read his face.

'Oh, I know that. But what are you doing here?'

He shrugged. 'My patch. Hobdoy's, just round the corner. What about you?'

'Well, I suppose I'm lost in a way. Not that it matters.'

She wished he would sit down. There was something tentative about his presence.

'Cairo University there,' he said. 'Botanical Gardens there. And the Zoo.'

'Oh, I remember seeing the Zoo. You weren't there last night?'

'Not my scene. I say, would you like a drink?'

'I don't even know what time it is. Actually, I'm rather hungry.'

He took his hands out of his pockets. His grin was disarming.

'Food and drink both. This way. If you'd like to.'

'Yes. Yes, thank you. I would. Very much.'

It must have been well past noon. Early afternoon. The shadows in the square had settled like animals, the boys melted away, a gardener with a broken rake slept curled under a flowering bush.

'Shouldn't you be working or something?'

46

'Close at two. Open at five. Depending.' Niki raised the counter-flap to let Charlotte through to the back room behind Hobdoy's small office. He stood, narrow shoulders hunched, shifted from one foot to the other. 'Well.'

Charlotte smiled to herself. Was he really so shy? Had he forgotten why he had brought her here – or was now regretting having done so? The shutters were closed but in the pale amber light that leaked through the louvres she could make out a low divan with a rug flung over it, the golden blink of beaten brass, clothes in a heap on the floor. A slatted wooden collapsible chair and a cheap picnic table, formica on metal legs. The remains of several meals, bottles, dirty plates, books everywhere. A couple of small pictures that might be old or good or both, a travel poster of Leningrad, yellowed and curling up at the corner. Then movement. A mole-coloured cat with paler muzzle jumped from its nest on the divan and complained.

Niki picked it up. From his arms it regarded Charlotte with blue-eyed suspicion.

'Firdus,' Niki said.

'Firdus?'

'The greatest whore in Egyptian history. Nina Fahmi gave her to me. Vodka?'

'Fine.'

'And there's some bread somewhere. And goat cheese. It was rather good. Sit down. Shove off, Firdus. Here.' He pulled the rug over greasy-looking pillows and opened the shutters.

'You live here then?'

'Most of the time.'

He put down a straight vodka in a beaker on the brass table by the divan and rummaged in a small fridge.

'Ah, yes. Bit ripe. Think it'll still do. Sorry, no plate.'

'That's all right.'

'I could wash one.' He scratched his head.

'No, really.'

47

Niki drew up the wooden chair and took a deep swallow of vodka.

'Well, what about Egypt?'

Charlotte thought.

'I don't know. Everyone keeps telling me what it is. D'you know what I mean?' The goat cheese was not bad at all.

'Oh yes. Don't listen, that's all.'

'You're not going to tell me?'

Niki shook his head. 'Lord, no.' He looked shocked.

Charlotte laughed.

'But that's your job, isn't it? An agent?'

He said lightly: 'I think Hobdoy's have forgotten me. Maybe just as well. I mean, they pay me but I'm probably a tax loss or something. What were you doing in the square?' He had very pale lashes, chapped knuckles.

'Running away? Looking round. I liked it. How long have you lived in Cairo?'

'A few years.'

'Did Hal say you were Russian?' She wondered about the Leningrad poster.

'Name only. Born in Hampstead.'

Charlotte could tell he didn't care for questions about himself. He was still drinking the vodka as if it were water but with no apparent effect. Oddly, she felt comfortable with him. She put aside her glass and walked around the room. Through the window a small courtyard. Shutters were closed. No movement. No sound. Egypt slept.

Most of Niki's books were in heaps but a few were ranged on a home-made shelf. A life of Tolstoy. *The Desert Fathers*, Thomas Browne's *Urn Burial*. One thick paperback, well-thumbed, pages turned down at the corners.

'*The Book of the Dead?*'

'Yes.'

His long arm came around her and as he plucked the book from the shelf Charlotte thought, what if I turned round and took that tired face in my hands? (Always a sucker for tramps, Leo would say.)

48

Charlotte took her place again on the divan. Firdus gave her the blue stare but allowed herself to be scratched under the chin, though the end of her tail twitched.

Niki read quietly, with hardly an inflection, as if he knew it by heart.

'In a clean place shall I sit on the ground beneath the foliage of the date palm.'

He flicked to another turned-down page.

'May I eat therein, may I drink . . . plough . . . reap . . . fight . . . make love.'

'Beautiful,' she said and he nodded vaguely.

'You know, of course. They were absolutely terrified of death. That's what it was all about – the hymns, the prayers, the poetry, the tombs, the temples, the mummification. Look. Where is it? Yes. "I shall not decay, I shall not rot, I shall not see corruption." Shouting in the dark.'

'Or they loved life? They must have.'

'Yes. Well.' Niki closed the book but did not move. 'Both could be true. Death's a dirty word nowadays, isn't it? We shove it away. Different reaction but same motive. It makes nonsense of life, everything. We're simply not here long enough. How do you live like that, under sentence of death?' His tone seemed calmly interested, objective. In a moment he might apologise for his intensity.

'I think, perhaps you have to live as if you won't die. I don't see any other way.'

(Phoebe's blazing love of life, Egypt, and then what? In the night. A cry she had taken to be a jackal, the sound of secrecy and anger, the flowers slapped down by bare feet? Alex away. Her first thought would have been the children. Was the knife honed and quick?)

Charlotte said: 'I've no idea what time it is. I forgot my watch. I suppose I'll have to get back.'

Niki seemed to wake up.

'Did someone say you were researching the Duncan killing?'

'Not exactly researching. You've heard of it? D'you know anything about it?'

He shook his head.

'A lot of people have heard of it. A famous story. Just some of the facts have been lost. Or put away. Or the reasons. Someone must remember. This place is a sort of oubliette, if that's what you want.'

Charlotte remembered Nina Fahmi.

'I've been warned not to look. I don't know why. I haven't really sorted the papers. Maybe there'll be time on the river.' She paused, trying to find the words. She wanted to explain to someone. 'I think Phoebe was a remarkable woman.' Charlotte smiled. 'It's funny. She's been dead so long and yet she's so vivid, more real than I feel. I might get mixed up with her so that I can't get out. That's crazy, of course.'

'I don't think so.'

On an impulse Charlotte said, her hand on the door: 'Before we leave Cairo, you wouldn't come out with me to Heliopolis? I expect the house has gone but I'd like to see.'

'Of course.'

'Only if you feel like it. I wouldn't know how to find it and Leo would be bored. Hal would say I was off my head.'

In the street the traffic had begun to move again. A couple of cabs dashed past.

'They're not going to stop. What do we do?'

'Shout.' Niki grinned. 'I couldn't get a cab once. I tried Arabic, French, everything. I was a bit pissed so I gave Swahili a go. Of which I know exactly five words. Worked. Ah, here we are.'

On the drive back Charlotte thought she had come a long way on her walk but as it turned out, it had not been very far at all.

Leo was flat out on the bed.

'I'm bushed.'

'Was it interesting?'

50

'Fantastic. Adila got us into the new diggings.'

Charlotte kicked off her canvas shoes.

'I thought you were going with Masoud?'

'Masoud and Adila. Didn't I say? She's got the contacts with the Department of Antiquities. Saw Hal on the way back.'

'Lord, not another party.' Charlotte poured them both a weak Scotch and soda. She went to the bathroom and came back. 'I have to keep remembering to clean my teeth with mineral water.'

'No. I said we'd eat in tonight.' He closed his eyes then opened them to say: 'What about you? Good day?'

Charlotte was changing. She stood in bra and pants, wondering about a shower. Adila, she thought. Do I mind?

'I went for a walk.'

'A walk? In Cairo? You must be mad.'

'No. It was interesting.'

'Didn't you hear about the bomb?'

'No. Where?'

'While you were walking wherever you walked, there was a bomb outside the Nile Hilton.'

'How awful. Was anyone hurt?' Charlotte reached into the wardrobe for the Liberty silk. The idea of a bomb seemed very distant.

'Didn't go off but Hal's full of theories. He says the new Revolution lot are more dangerous than the Fundamentalists. What they really want is Nasser back.'

'Nasser's dead.' Charlotte paused, decided against silk. 'Does Hal work for the CIA?'

Leo yawned. 'I should think so. I don't know. Does it matter?'

'No, it doesn't. It doesn't matter at all.'

They ate in the coffee-shop. Chicken and chips. Like an airport terminal, it was a place people seemed to be passing through, a limbo. Charlotte watched the people. Leo was talking about something Masoud had said. Some

51

interesting artifacts turning up in the Cairo market. From the Valley of the Kings and possibly Akhetaton. Leo was clearly excited.

'If there have been any finds to do with Akhenaton that would be sensational. They never discovered his tomb, you know, if he had one.'

'D'you think you should have been an archaeologist?'

'Maybe. Not sure. All that spadework, literally.' He grinned. 'Too impatient. Too much of a romantic. The same reasons I'm a journalist not a writer?'

Charlotte nodded.

'I forgot to ask. How were your hotels yesterday?'

'Oh God, yes. Sticking my head in the loos. Counting the Kleenex dispensers. Bad Cairo plumbing – you have to smell it to believe it. I have a sort of nightmare. The whole world done over by the Hiltons and the Sheratons and the Holiday Inns. In-house TV, giveaway bathcaps, that bubble bath that tears your skin off.'

'D'you have to work this time?'

'Might get by. I'll see. We're due a real holiday.' Leo signed the bill without reading it. 'Sorry, love. Not much of a life for you, is it?'

'It's what we agreed. I'm fine. I'm busy.' She put her hand on his. It was not like Leo to ask that sort of question. 'I do love you, you know.'

Walking away from the table Leo took her arm and bent to kiss her cheek.

On their way back to their room they passed the reception counter and Charlotte heard herself summoned.

'Missis Hamp!' The clerk was waving an envelope.

'Thank you.'

Leo went to bed at once but Charlotte took the envelope to the table she had been using as a desk.

The covering note written with a cheap biro on Hobdoy's paper was from Niki Yussoupov: 'Been fishing in the oubliette – hope this helps.' Clipped to the note was a photocopied cutting for November 1924, from the

Egyptian Gazette. Considering the subject matter, it was surprisingly brief.

TRAGIC INCIDENT AT ASWAN

Death by Night

Murderous native assassins, believed to be Nubians, two days ago broke into the house of the popular Captain Alexander Duncan on Elephantine Island. Here they slaughtered his wife, Mrs Phoebe Duncan, and young son, Robin, and made their escape by night.

Captain Duncan served under our present High Commissioner, Field Marshal (then General) Allenby in Sinai. He has worked since he resigned his commission first as a representative of the Cairo City Police in Aswan and since the end of the Protectorate as Intelligence Officer.

It is generally believed that this was a single act perpetrated by natives crazed from the effects of the cocaine or Hashish now so regrettably introduced by cynical Greek and Armenian scoundrels intent on undermining the decency of your average Egyptian and his long-held respect for all the benefits the English have brought to his country.

Your reporter has it on the highest authority that no connection is suspected between this single act of crazed treachery and the cowardly assassination on the 19th of this month in Cairo of Sir Lee Stack, Commander-in-Chief of the Egyptian Army and Governor-General of the Sudan.

At the time of the incident Captain Duncan was away, carrying out his sometimes perilous duties in Khartoum. Mercifully, his infant daughter, Pansy, survived, hidden in a closet by a faithful native servant.

Captain 'Sandy' Duncan (as he is known among his many friends at the Gezira Club) is assured of the outrage and sympathy of the entire British community in Egypt.

Charlotte would have liked coffee but to call room service might wake Leo. She poured herself a Coke and lit a cigarette. She worked until the sky was coloured by the beautiful pink smog of the Cairo dawn. She heard the parp of the first traffic, pulled a wrap round her shoulders and walked through the foyer and the open doors. Early travellers, waiting for transport, yawned. She looked out over the city – at this time of day beautiful – and hearing the now familiar call of the muezzin, understood for the first time properly, Leo's passion. To hold the past, still warm, in your hands. Yet, what she felt after her long night's work was more than that? Different, anyway. As though she had, that night, chosen to lose herself. Somewhere out there, in that vast country that had once been ocean, Phoebe turned and laughed and loved Egypt too much and died, her eyes wide open. Charlotte felt sure her eyes were open.

Life and death, such a slim margin, no deeper than a ditch, slim as a knife curved to the shape of a throat.

An early-morning walker was making his way crab-wise up the hill. Max Stiller waved. Charlotte waved back.

'No more talk about bombs!' Nina Fahmi threw up her hands. 'Tonight we are in my apartment. Positively no bombs!'

'OK, Nina,' Hal said, then he caught sight of Charlotte.

'You look stunning, Charlie.'

'Thank you.' Poor old Hal, she thought. What would it be like to be Hal alone, without his gang? She wondered if Niki would come.

Of course, there had been nothing at Heliopolis. Niki had turned up in an elderly Volkswagen, a complaining tin beetle with a hole in the floor. Charlotte had been surprised that he drove at all, even more surprised that he had come.

Where there had once been the small house in a garden under acacias on the edge of the desert, another new hotel was going up behind one of the large advertising hoardings that lined the road to the airport.

Aching from the drive, Charlotte was glad to walk. Here,

where Phoebe had written of apricots and wolves and vines and the cool breeze the City did not enjoy, there was dust and dirt and the skeleton of a building that gave the appearance of having been started and then abruptly abandoned. The desert was already reclaiming the site. A buckled Mercedes lay upside-down in a ditch.

'Are you sure we've got the right place?'

Niki nodded, his words lost as a fat jet grumbled its way into the sky. Another was circling, waiting to land. The first, now airborne, looked lighter, as though up there the battle with gravity were less serious.

Charlotte sat at the foot of a flight of concrete steps that led nowhere, in the shade. Niki, with his hands in his pockets, wandered through the building site. She saw him, a small figure, look up at a hoarding: *Arab Contractors Ltd*. He strolled, a frail-seeming diminishing shape between cement-mixers and cranes.

Away from the road, it was very quiet, still, the bump of the big jets distanced by some trick of sound. A quick flick of movement and Charlotte glanced down to see a small lizard freeze in its tracks, playing dead.

Phoebe's first mention of Nayra came in a letter to her sister dated July 1919, Heliopolis:

Darling Dorothy,

All kinds of news for you. First, we're going in the autumn to Aswan! You know I wanted that more than anything but didn't press A. The marvellous thing is, he wants it too. He could have got into Public Building or Finance, which are the plum Cairo jobs but instead he asked for some Police Department posting that means we can actually live in Aswan. No one else wants it so it wasn't very difficult. In fact a lot of people tried to persuade him against it but I'm proud to say he can be very stubborn when he wants to . . . not much money and rather vague duties. Not a policeman in the way you might think. More keeping an eye open, a sort of District Officer, he says.

Then at last I've made a real Egyptian friend – at least I think so. All through Rosemary Gilchrist – one of the Residency wives. She's not v. clever but nice and fun and just as bored as I was with the usual crowd. Can you believe it – harems still exist in a lot of the upper-class families! Rosemary told me, said would I like to see one.

Don't know what I expected. Fat ladies giggling and eating Turkish delight, I suppose, but it wasn't a bit like that. There were sweets and a nice sherbet drink as well as mint tea. No men, of course, but the women dressed in ordinary clothes . . . Rather stuffy room, over-furnished and at first I thought it was going to be stiff – polite questions and answers about nothing in particular. Family and clothes and so on. Lots of talk about shopping. Apparently they're not allowed to go into a shop in the ordinary way.

Then just as I'd decided it was a waste of time and I'd pass out if I didn't get some air I had a really good conversation with a girl called Nayra. Not exactly pretty but very bright intelligent eyes and we took to each other at once. She explained all sorts of things – about the black cloak they call the *izar* they have to wear outside the harem, and the veil. Nayra said there's a movement – a bit like our suffragettes, I suppose – to free women from the veil and all the restrictions. There's even some kind of association she belongs to for intellectual Egyptian women.

Anyway, we couldn't talk as long as I wanted to but sure we'll meet again. I promised to lend her books, though she's much cleverer than I am. Speaks French and English and some Turkish. Don't mean to make her sound a blue-stocking. She's very amusing. Could be *wicked*.

Sorry I've gone on again all about me . . . just beginning to learn a bit about Egypt makes me realise how much there is to learn, that there'll be no end to it.

Must stop. Even writing's exhausting in this heat. See now why almost everyone goes to Alexandria. Trouble is, I can't just lie around indoors, trying to stay cool. You know me. *Covered* in freckles. Try to bleach them with lemon. No luck so far.

Do hope you get to Florence in the autumn and Mother's

really over that rotten 'flu. It's terrible to think, the war to
end wars but people still dying. So many. Take care.

Love always and kisses,

Phoebe

Meeting Nayra Hazim. Felt at once we'd be friends for
ever . . . Alex pleased, I think. Rosemary G. driving me
home said something peculiar about not getting mixed up
in politics. Wouldn't explain. Not that I care. Nayra not
approved of for some reason? Don't want to quarrel with
Rosemary. But if I have to, I will.

'I'm afraid there was never much hope.'

'No, I realise that.'

As the beetle coughed into life, Niki reached one-handed
behind his bucket seat and produced a bottle of mineral
water.

'Unless you'd like something stronger?'

'Oh no.' Charlotte realised she was keeping him from his
bottle. 'It's what that newspaper report doesn't say. As if
Phoebe didn't count. Shouldn't you be at work?'

'Hobdoy's chugs along without me. Or not. No one misses
me, anyway. Damn.'

Charlotte was flung sideways in her seat as Niki fought to
slow the car. A Datsun van was crossing the mainstream
of traffic, carrying a camel.

Charlotte laughed. 'It looks so disdainful.'

Even after the passing of the camel the traffic appeared
unable to get going again.

As the Volkswagen coughed, choked and finally came to
life again, Charlotte said: 'I think I know what happened.
She broke the rules.'

Nina Fahmi's apartment was a weird mixture of Maples
repro circa 1950 and a magpie's collection of objects:
onyx, a gold serpent bracelet that should probably have
been in the Cairo museum, a silver-framed photograph of

57

fat old Farouk on the deck of a motor-yacht. Charlotte peered more closely at his entourage – some sitting at his feet, some standing, all laughing. Nina, a slim, dark pretty woman, clearly recognisable; looking down at her from the shadow of an awning, a tall man.

'Ah,' said Nina,' there you are, my darling girl! Forgive this place – such a muddle. One lives too long. Death would be a good thing, to shake off the clutter.'

'Is that your husband?' Charlotte asked.

Tonight Nina was disguised as a parrot. Something silk covered in layered feathers with a feather-trimmed hem. An acid-green boa and more feathers on top of her head fixed to a jewelled clip. Amazingly, she looked wonderful.

'Oh yes. That would be when? 1950? Dear Fahmi was a Copt, a true Egyptian, not one of the monkey invaders. Always he was in despair at these Arabs. He had a little cross, you know, tattooed inside his wrist. And we had a lovely house and Christmas. And the big streets were so clean then! Do you think I should get rid of this terrible piano? I cannot bear the thought that it might outlive me! Such possessions are ageing, are they not, like children. Not that we had any. My pelvis was considered too small and I can't say I was sorry. And you, my dear, do you have any?'

'Children? No, we haven't.' Nina's beady eyes continued to enquire. Charlotte said lightly: 'That is, I've had a few miscarriages. Oh, look, there's Dr Stiller. I must speak to him.'

'Forgive a nosy old woman.' Nina did not wait for Charlotte. She forgave herself and chattered on. 'Now you'll be very careful on that filthy river? And you'll come and see me at my little house at Aswan? We may even meet at Luxor. Masoud and I usually break the journey there.'

'Masoud?'

Nina flapped her paws.

'Oh, I know he's naughty with his boy friends but I think this horrid AIDS has given him a good fright. And

for an old woman a wicked pédé is company. Ah, Max!
You are a bad boy too. You have neglected me for
your museums.'

Nina chattered off. Max smiled.

'I've just had an interesting talk with your husband about
the Osman theory.'

'Oh yes, I haven't seen you since. You were going to visit
the mummy. Did you look on the face of Joseph?'

Max shrugged.

'I saw the face of a man who died 3,400 years ago. He
did not tell me his name. Perhaps it does not matter so
much who was the first monotheist – Moses or Akhenaton.'
His face looked heavy then he brightened. 'But you and
your quest? That is much more interesting. Are you
any further?'

Charlotte said: 'Niki Yussoupov found me a newspaper
cutting. That's all, really. Somehow, I get the feeling that
the deeper I go the more complicated it will become. Or
there'll be a blank wall. Nothing. If I could stand back it
would be like a thriller – a detective story – but I can't.'

Max nodded. There was a buzz around the long sofa. Hal
was booming.

'Charlie, come here. They won't believe me.'

'Won't believe what?'

'The Nile's falling. There'll be a drought by July and that's
curtains for Egypt. Back to the desert.'

'Hal's exaggerating as usual, Mrs Hamp.' Adila did
not approve. Charlotte was mildly interested, not so
much in the prophecy of drought as in the girl's attitude.
Educated, intelligent, travelled, yet in Adila's Egypt there
was no poverty, the Nile would never dry up. What
would she have said if the bomb had gone off? She
gazed gravely at Hal from the arm of the sofa where
she perched. Still young enough to look pretty when she
frowned. 'It is simply that Lake Nasser is a little low
in spite of the floods in the Sudan. Nothing to worry
about.'

Adila moved away. Hal took Charlotte's hand and drew her down to take the girl's place on the arm of the sofa.

'And they're trying to make the desert bloom. Did you know, Charlie? Pioneer farmers sweating it out in that godawful sand. They just forgot to plant windbreaks. The American University's on to it now. You met old Ted Southby and Marietta? Canadians. He's been consulting. They're coming on the *Hathor*.'

Charlotte said: 'Hal, if you despise the Egyptians so much why do you live here?'

The grin was not quite wiped from his face.

'I always forget, Charlie. You're pretty sharp when you want to be.' He was slightly drunk but his pale eyes were entirely sober. 'The thing about the Egyptians is, once you've caught on that they're kids, that's fine. Great guys. I tell you, no one loves them more than I do.'

'That's an incredibly patronising attitude. What's more, I don't think you believe it.'

There was just a flicker in Hal's eyes, enough to make Charlotte think: he's the one playing games. Then he was genial again.

'And what about you old imperialist British? Who did the patronising then? You think the Egyptians love the Brits?'

'No, I don't.' (They slit my great-aunt's throat and she loved them.) Charlotte bit her lip. 'Guilty, no doubt. All I mean, Hal, is that the empires are finished. But you haven't answered my question. Why do you stay?'

'Maybe I like the climate? Nowhere else to go?'

'Home?'

He said quite soberly: 'And where in the world is that, Charlie? You tell me, I'll go.'

Hal's words brought to mind, of all people, Niki Yussoupov with his plimsolls and his cat and his funny English manners, reading from *The Book of the Dead* in the scruffy room behind Hobdoy's. Charlotte looked around for him but was snatched away by Nina to

60

talk to a very short Dutch agronomist who nodded sharply as at a well-meaning student and explained at great length the peculiar problems attached to the agriculturalisation of the desert, these including not only the quantity of sand – of which he clearly disapproved – but also the Egyptian temperament, at once impulsive and easily downcast.

Bending to listen, Charlotte felt like Alice.

'So what you mean,' she said, 'is that if they had too much water instead of sand, and the Egyptians were Dutch, it would be all right?'

She talked to another agronomist – the tall, elderly Canadian Hal had mentioned, one of the couple she had seen at St Sergius, quiet, courteous, a little deaf, and anxious to introduce her to his wife.

'Oh well,' said Charlotte, 'I expect we'll meet again,' as the party surged between them and she found herself carried on the tide to the fringe. She felt as she had that first night at Hal Douglas's, as though she were standing outside watching through a window. Leo had said once fondly, amused: you're a sort of spy, aren't you, the way you watch.

'Sorry? What did you say?'

Leo grinned.

'Hal wants to take a bottle to Niki Yussoupov's. You coming?'

'No. Bit whacked. You go.'

Surprisingly, Leo shook his head.

'Me too. Sandwich and sleep. We've got the river tomorrow.'

'Oh yes, of course. I'd forgotten. The river.'

In the cab Leo tried and failed to stretch his long legs.

'Nina's incredible,' he said. 'She looked as if she wanted plucking. What was that row with Hal?'

'Not a row.'

'It was from where I stood. Never known Hal lost for words. What's going on?'

The cab had stopped and the driver was yelling into the

61

darkness. He turned back to Charlotte and Leo, shrugged and pointed.

Leo craned to look.

'Some sort of road-block or check-point. Or just Cairo traffic. And it's raining again.'

A figure in thick, prickly khaki appeared at the cab window. The rain streamed down the barrel of his rifle. He talked to the driver then thrust his head and shoulders inside. His frown became a grin.

'German?'

'English.'

It seemed to be a disappointment that they were English. The frown came back along with some appalling French mixed with Arabic. Charlotte sat back. It passed through her mind that he could force them from the cab and shoot them there in the dark rain and Egypt would go on and life would go on. Should she be afraid?

'Can you make out what he's saying?'

The driver's single contribution had been to turn up his radio.

Leo had been straining to understand. Now he laughed.

'What's the joke?'

'Cigarettes. For God's sake give him your cigarettes.'

'There's only three left.'

'Whatever.'

Charlotte handed over the packet and, for good measure, the disposable lighter. The soldier, or whatever he was, leaned further in and shook hands with them both. He stepped back, waved his hand, and the cab driver went into a U-turn.

'Long way round,' Leo said. 'Some scare. You all right?'

'Fine.'

Just as they turned she glimpsed the red-and-white-striped pole across the road. She had seen many such poles before, marking the end of one country and the beginning of another.

*

'Did you know Masoud was gay?'

Leo was coming out of the bathroom, pulling off his tie.

'Never thought about it. Yes, I suppose he might be. Not to notice.'

She was sitting at the desk-table. He put his arms round her shoulders and Charlotte raised her face and leaned back against him.

'Coming to bed?' Leo said.

'Mnn. In a bit.'

'Soon.' He kissed her cheek.

Their luggage for the river was half-packed. There would be time in the morning.

As Charlotte moved the heavy table-lamp, the roses shuddered and spilled a petal. She spread out the thick wallet-files. In her work the other morning she had more or less sorted them. The letters her father had so assiduously (lovingly?) preserved; the cheap notebooks with navy marbled covers in which Phoebe had kept her occasional journals. (And who had saved those? Alex? The servant Amir?)

Charlotte flicked through the pages. A reference (repeated somewhere in the letters) to Alex's impatience with Anglo-Egyptian bureaucratic muddles. A line drawing of a lotus column. Another, less careful and more lively, of Arab children playing. A third, of a girl, clearly Egyptian though not veiled, holding a fair-haired infant in her arms. Beneath the last there was scribbled in a quick hand: *Saiza and Pansy*.

There were a number of such sketches scattered throughout the journals and letters. A few in the letters had clearly been done for Dorothy's only child, Howard. Captions read: *Uncle Alex on a camel. Both cross.* Then: *Kitten, present from Nayra, Saiza don't like!*

Charlotte closed the files for packing, then on impulse pulled out a stiffened envelope that held the only pictures she had of Phoebe. The small pastel portrait – lacking entirely the amateur vigour of her own drawings – of the

63

girl with the same impossible, crinkly auburn hair and fair skin, grey eyes as Charlotte. She was sitting very properly, wearing a silk shawl, but even the portraitist, striving to capture or, failing capture, to invent, a conventional beauty, could not entirely suppress the air of barely contained impatience: as if the subject might at any second break out of the picture, into life.

And then there was a photograph of a young woman wearing white, in a felucca under sail. She did not know she was being photographed. Her face was shadowed by a sun-hat, turned away from the camera, dipped, violet-shaded. The picture had been faded by sun and time and the light, in the first place, had been too bright.

4

All aboard the *Hathor*.

'What about this then, Charlie?'

On deck Charlotte shivered and pulled her shawl about her but her arms were still cold and her high heels felt unsafe.

'I don't know yet, Hal. Wonderful, I think. Are those ruins?'

'Brickworks. Miles of them. How d'you like the little old lady?'

'The what? Oh, the boat. Nice. Better than those big cruise things.'

'Quarter of a century, she's done. Cabin OK?'

'Fine.'

'I'll turn in then.'

Hal kissed her cheek. Charlotte leant on the rail. The banks of the Nile slid past. There was a shout of laughter from the brightly lit bar. It was too soon for social groupings to have formed (though the French had already demanded a table for themselves) but there was Hal's crowd, of course, and within it Leo and the other travel writers who knew each other and were drinking together. At dinner Charlotte had watched, amused, guessing at nationalities, wondering about relationships, speculating on the chances of civilisation surviving the unavoidable intimacy of fifty people voyaging for three weeks and 600 miles on a vessel so small.

'What's funny?' Leo had asked.

'Just wondering how long it will take for war to break out.'

She had noticed the elderly Canadian couple and looked for

Max but failed to find him. Someone said he was eating in his cabin. She hoped he was all right.

In the narrow cabin there was an old-fashioned fan that probably didn't work. The window was a rectangle covered with mesh against mosquitoes.

'What was all that at El Wasta this morning?'

'Eh? All what?'

Leo was having difficulty undressing in such a small space. Charlotte put a finger in her book, then closed it. She couldn't concentrate anyway.

'Hal. Didn't you notice? He seemed fussed.'

It had been suddenly, surprisingly hot. Drinking black tea under the awning Charlotte had marvelled at the capacity of the *Hathor* – how she could swallow so many gallons of bottled water, haunches of unidentifiable animal wrapped in muslin, crates of booze and planters' peanuts. There had been a drama on the gang-plank about luggage. What she had taken for crew were not crew after all but land-men haggling over tips. And then a military-looking jeep had screeched up, scattering dogs and children and hens and porters and Hal had gone into conference with what appeared to be an official in the front passenger-seat. By the time he came back on board he was sweating.

'Oh, that,' Leo said. 'Another scare or probably the same one. Someone upstairs didn't want us to sail. Poor old Hal. If we hadn't, he might have lost his cut. Nothing to worry about anyway.'

Cairo, September 1919

Mother, you are not to worry, please! It is so different if you are in the country, as we are, one doesn't think of awful things that might happen but almost certainly won't. You say Alex's job at Aswan sounds mysterious. I expect that's because I'm muddle-headed and don't quite know what it is myself. But the only danger is that he might get bored! Not that he'll miss the clubs that much, any more than I'll miss those awful Residency tea-parties. We are of the same mind there – as we are in everything. He'll be glad too to get away from the Cairo talk against Allenby. (Sorry to hear the spiteful gossip has reached England.) All the Dodos say Egypt needs a firmer hand but few of them know Allenby as Alex does and even fewer know anything at all about the Egyptians.

Please don't bother yourself to send out the things you mention. The china would probably get broken and since I won't have to do the sort of official entertaining that goes on in Cairo, I plan to live very simply. No damask tablecloths! Would be glad of more books though – one crate went astray at Suez.

Must stop. Packing to do. Yes, I have gallons of quinine. Am trying to learn Arabic but although I have a few more words now, don't think I'm ever going to master the script.

Once we leave Cairo the post will not be at all reliable. So if you don't hear for a while please don't imagine I've been eaten by a crocodile! I haven't even seen one yet . . . Anyway, it looks now as if we shan't get away until after Christmas.

Leo snored. Charlotte, sleepless, switched on her dim bedhead light and reached in the locker for one of the wallet files. She knew them now by touch. In the morning she must find somewhere safe to keep them. Since they came aboard the feeling had grown upon her of time as something liquid, contiguous. So that she can sit here, propped against a hard pillow while the dark banks sleep and the *Hathor* noses her way south, carefully seeking the ever-changing channels, trailing her quiet wake behind her; and at the same time Phoebe wakes in the sleeping house at Heliopolis, pulls a wrap over her nightdress (autumn now), sits down to write – keeping the lamp turned low, not to disturb Amir.

She is still very young; that is, she refuses to qualify experiences, impressions, her hunger. At this stage, she is ravenous to live.

Journal, September 1919, Heliopolis
A real adventure at last! To the Khan el Khalili bazaar with Nayra, both disguised in the black cloth native women

67

wear in the street – and veil. Cheap, poor material so
that no one can take us for grand ladies. Suspect Ahmed
approves and doesn't approve. Nayra said he'd sent a
servant to follow us but gave him the slip . . . Not
that anything at all exciting happened to us. Quite the opposite!
No one saw us. See what Nayra means. It really is the
veil of invisibility. Both got the giggles. Back to Nayra's where
Ahmed was waiting. Quite cross because we were late
and he was worried. Funny. He's working secretly for the
Wafd. Supposed to mean liberation for everyone but doesn't
like his own sister going shopping . . . I rather took to
him. Young, sense of humour. Hope I'll see him again. N. says
when she was a child and they went to Paris her mother
wouldn't let her go into the department stores. So they bought
all the magazines and a servant had to do the shopping
from pictures . . . Don't understand. Probably never will. Even
royal Princesses support the women's movement. But in
Nayra's house male visitors must still talk to women through a
wooden grille.

Such good talks with Nayra. About everything. The 'Revolution' in March. Sounds much worse than I had realised. Felt
ashamed that I was in the country yet so ill-informed about
what was going on. Seems that when demonstrating peacefully
the women (who came from all classes and religions) were
treated brutally by our soldiers. All I'd heard was that two or
three were hurt – the implication that it was their own fault.
Now I know many hurt, some wounded, a few killed.

I've been so naïve! No doubt a conspiracy to hide the worst
from the women – particularly from the young bride! . . .

Faced Alex. Almost a row, our first. Said I want him to hide
nothing from me. That was our promise. No secrets. Made up,
of course. Can never quarrel with him for long.

A. blames not just German-Turkish plots from before war
but insensitivities in administration. If there were more like
him there'd be no problem!

Still stick to what I told Mother. Convinced if treated
properly the Egyptians feel a bond with us. A sort of love.
Nothing will ever shake me from that opinion.

Late now. So much to get down. Why? Why write about
it? For myself, I suppose, since no one else will ever read this.

Because I need to write it. Because Rosemary Gilchrist has
decided she is my best friend and is trying to pump me.
Hoping I'm up to something she can gossip about. She'll never
know what I really think any more than I'd tell her about
Nayra and Ahmed, what they really do . . . Just something I
must write down because I want to. That is, I think it's
better to risk and make mistakes. To trust. That's it. That's
all.

In Heliopolis Phoebe blotted the page, locked away the
journal, and snuffed out the lamp while Charlotte lay down,
listened to the shush of water fingering the hull, the muted,
regular beat of the engine, and slid into furry sleep.

Max Stiller slept thinly in the inferior double cabin on the
lower deck allotted to him as a single. All night he heard
the strange voices of the vessel: a sound like someone being
beaten, the terrible monotony, as insistent as a sounding
clock, of the engine turning over.

Night thoughts. Half-dreams. The pills not working so well
now.

Old fool, what am I doing here? Why Egypt for a voyage
to death?

Because, meanwhile, there is still life?

'Family?' the doctor had said.

For a messenger of death he had been offensively young,
dressed for squash or whatever Americans play in winter.
(Well, why not? Should he have torn his robes, daubed his
cheeks with ash?) He had sat with his back to the light. On his
desk one sprig of winter jasmine. A silver-framed photograph
of a woman with two children announced: I am human, too.
His tone was that of a dentist explaining in matter-of-fact
tones that an infected molar was past repair. Soon, quite
soon, the body will have to go but not to worry. Better
without it, in the long run.

'Family?' Max had echoed. 'Oh, yes, family.' You could
plant a forest from my family.

'If you would like me to. If there is anyone it would be helpful. Speak to.'

If you can call up the dead, yes.

'Thank you. I think not.'

Max had a flash of gallows laughter, suppressed but only just. The Connecticut snow fell outside. The young doctor was struggling so hard to earn his preposterous wage, which would, with any luck, be met by the university upon whose campus Max had spontaneously started to die.

Felt a twinge at the Dean's party and excused himself abruptly. They had probably thought him drunk and doubted their wisdom in importing this small, balding Englishman who was failing to be distinguished. Left the room in hiccups, terrible colour. Raised eyebrows and a helping hand he refused. Only a couple of hundred yards across the campus to his small room. A few flakes of snow idled in the mid-air. Max felt at his back the inquisitive silence he had left behind him.

Then the true fall had come as he was addressing the Creative Writing Workshop. All those eager upturned young faces like nestlings waiting to be fed (make me a writer, teach me the trick, I want it now) and Max had opened his mouth to speak, gasped, doubled up and tumbled: a slow fall, a stage fall almost. So nothing was broken. Dragging his chair after him Max was simply floored. So positions were reversed. His was the upturned face, theirs were the shocked, enquiring beaks crowded around him.

In that cold climate Max felt disapproved of. He had become death, an obscene reminder that for all their courtesy, they could not wait to pack up and off. Not certain, of course, but a possibility had become a probability, better gently parcelled up and despatched with a sonic boom east, away.

A pretty girl asked if she could help him pack.

'You'll be better at home.'

Her hair fell across her face as she bent to lift up his small suitcase. Her skin was appallingly clear, her teeth had known the attentions of the best orthodontist. She should not be exposed to his mortality.

'Home? Oh, yes. Indeed. Thank you. There's no need.'

'I'm really sorry,' she said and he knew she was. Max would carry that bright, concerned, unlived face in his mind at least halfway across the Atlantic, a candle to light him home to bed.

But now, instead of dying in Connecticut or in mid-Atlantic or in England, or Jerusalem, Max is waking up in Egypt.

Dawn comes cold at 6 a.m. Max, rising to obey his insistent bladder, is a long time peeing without much satisfaction, in elderly spasms and drips. Wrapping a blanket around his shanks, he blinks and nods at the shore. Where time does an acrobatic flip and, planning his canal, stands Joseph. Exile, captive, Pharaoh's bailiff, keeper of the granaries, Israelite made good among the Egyptians. The Pharaoh who knew not Joseph waits to be born. Meanwhile the Bahr Yusuf canal takes steady, clever shape in the head of the alien who will water a little, at least, of the desert. If story is history and history truth.

And as Max Stiller waves, the son of Israel from the land of Canaan shades his brow against the sun rising in the east and imagines the passing of the *Hathor*. And salutes.

The breakfast gong sounded at last. Max rinsed out the taste of the night with the pink stuff from the plastic bottle, put in his teeth, reached for the first pill of the day from among his pharmacopia. He scraped at his grey stubble with soap and razor. Shaving: a young man's game.

He nicked his chin. The blood hesitated then spurted. He reached for the cotton wool and shuffled off to breakfast. Max Stiller still.

Leo slept on. Charlotte dressed and slipped out soon after dawn. A cup of watery Nescafé with Longlife milk in the dining-room served by stern Nubians in important galabiyas. Then, on the still empty deck she sat in a gauzy, chilly, early light. The tick-tack of a water wheel, an invisible donkey braying. The gauze turned to scarves, streamers, the sun

71

came through and there, laid out for her it seemed, was a moving picture of another Egypt. Houses of red mud brick, a narrow, cultivated strip of brilliant green. The blue-green of palms, the yellow-green of crops.

It was the ship that was moving, not the land. Illusion.

Then the donkey moved, one figure then another waved, waist-high in green. The amplified radio-call of the muezzin and at the water's edge an old man for whom the passing of the *Hathor* was nothing, prostrated himself full-length to the east. He looked as though he were worshipping the earth.

A child ran down to the water and waved.

Charlotte waved back.

There was warmth in the sun now. It closed her eyes. She dozed.

Feet. Voices.

'Last time I was in Outer Mongolia.'

'They're banning package tours in the Seychelles. Did you know?'

'The fixed-price bazaar at Luxor.'

Adila's small but curiously carrying voice telling an audience in the stern what they must see, how they must see it.

Then Charlotte was snapped fully awake and the elderly Canadian woman, the agronomist's wife, was grinning like a monkey from the next lounger. She wore dungarees, track shoes, a straw solar topee with a mirror in the brim and two sets of spectacles on gold chains round her neck.

'You don't mind?'

'No. Of course.'

'My name's Marietta Southby, haven't we met? We went to the Galapagos last year. I do recommend the Galapagos. Nepal a couple of times. The children wanted us to cancel because of the hijack but I said and Ed agrees, when you've got to go that's your time and it could be the last chance for Egypt? Have you done the Cape to Cairo? No? Well, that's two months, of course and Ed's not too happy about a war zone? Though isn't everywhere over here a war zone now? Have you noticed, the Japanese have cancelled en bloc?

72

My son's a dentist? Well, I said to Ed the children don't realise life's not a rehearsal, this is all we get, he's had two heart-bypasses and a prostate and he's good as new, he keeps his weight down and there's my brother-in-law in Florida playing golf with the old folk and eaten to pieces with rodent cancer? Anyhow we'd had our shots? I hope you've had your shots, dear, and don't ever take ice and clean your teeth with bottled water and no salads? And the fruit, the water gets up through the roots even if you peel it? There's that nice couple up from the famine from the Sudan on their honeymoon and all they had was one iced juice at the Hilton? We're booked for the Amazon in the fall I always say it's so interesting to meet people, you never know who you'll get, I think I recognise that gentleman who wasn't in the dining-room last night but I can't put my finger on it and the two Australian girls who took the optional to Sinai? Don't they buzz around? There's an author aboard, I think, had you heard, and of course all Hal's crowd so interesting, that sweet, poor starved courier boy from Hobdoy's? And where is your handsome husband? Last time we were in Kom Ombo I'd skip the mummified crocodiles if I were you like a lot of old handbags? Well, it's been so interesting to talk to you dear, you should cover up, that complexion, did you know there's an undertaker on board incognito so to speak? Not that we'll need his services? We came on the *Hathor* before oh years and years ago, Philae was underwater then before they moved it, the cow goddess but you know that, and love and fun, well you just say if there's anything Ed or I we must all help each other, Lomotil or Immodium, I do recommend Haag but Fodor not so much and as for the Blue Guide, oh I see you've got it? Anything, anything at all, see you again, we're all in the same boat aren't we?'

Marietta spotted Ed – the thin and amiable-looking half-retired agronomist, remarkably wiry for a heart case – and without waiting for a reply from Charlotte, called his name, raised a happy claw and scuttered over to him. He was wearing a green eye shade. As Charlotte watched their

73

reunion – the way Marietta hooked her arm through his, he bent smiling, proud of her, glad to see her, straightening his shoulders like a groom with a pretty bride – she thought: there is love. We talk about it too much, carve it up with knives and forks and there it is, quite simply, love.

As the morning advanced the heat sucked the colour from the sky. The land came fully to life (for them, Charlotte thought, we are the moving picture). Adila finished her lecture. Leo had surfaced and was reading in the shade. Hal and the travel writers (excepting Leo) already had a drinking party going in the bar. A ferry crossed carrying a load of affronted camels from one side to the other, reminding Charlotte of the Datsun van at Heliopolis. On the bank Charlotte saw a woman hitch up her black robe. Underneath she wore a flowered cotton dress. Beyond the green there were glimpses of the eastern desert to port, the Libyan to starboard. The borderline between the busily cultivated strip and the sand that nourished no one and nothing was as precise as the demarcation between life and death.

Phoebe had said something like that in the journal notes on the winter voyage to Aswan. (Are these my eyes or hers?). Some sketches of life on the Nile for her young relations.

A wonderful lethargy . . . so lazy, dreamy. Alex to myself. If it could go on for ever. Temples wonderful but it's the river. Miss Nayra but she'll write, she'll come. Nothing else. Peace, not to step ashore. Ever again.

Immortality – like this? Desert beautiful, dangerous. A. teasing me about scorpions.

Feel suspended between lives.

On one scrap of paper a line drawing of a fat, black-robed woman carrying a pitcher on her head. Captioned for her nieces and nephews: *'Oops! Couldn't do it. Could you?'*

And looking up, Charlotte saw there was the woman, though the pitcher was of some metal nowadays, no longer clay. And the children – so many children – running down to the water, not only waving now but shouting. Calling back

74

hello (though she could not possibly be heard), Charlotte felt that for a second she had entered the picture. Which was probably by no means as picturesque as it appeared. Hard, short lives. Herodotus's famous gift of the Nile so trumpeted in the brochure featuring Ramses II and Hosni Mubarak, apparently about to be withdrawn. Not yet. There's still the water buffalo and the donkey turning the wheel. What becomes of them, those calling children?

'Ah, the children.'

Max lowered himself into the cane chair by Charlotte's lounger. Charlotte noticed he had nicked himself shaving. He still wore the blob of cotton wool.

'We missed you at dinner last night?'

'I decided to forgo the joys of Egyptian cooking.' Max raised his hand, ordered Turkish coffee for two from the waiter smoking deep in the shade of the awning. 'However, I have not been wasting my time this morning. Did you know that we have on board, among others, a honeymoon couple, a midwife, a pathologist, an undertaker and a taxidermist? Everything we might need from birth to death, including mummification. But who is who, do you suppose? It is interesting to speculate.' His pebble spectacles glinted wickedly.

Charlotte laughed.

'How on earth do you know?'

'I pay,' said Max calmly. 'A little chat with the boat manager.' He accepted the Turkish coffee he knew he should not be drinking. 'Shukran, Mohammed.'

'But why?'

'You will find that the last instinct to go is curiosity. Now, for instance, with all of Egypt around and before us, I am wondering about that very English gentleman on the side-deck there. The panama hat, the trousers so immaculately pressed, the silk scarf at the neck. One could invent for him a whole history of the correct school, university, regiment, wife, family, opinions. You see the signet ring on the little finger? You take him to be what he appears?'

75

'Yes,' Charlotte smiled. 'But obviously he isn't. You sound like Hercule Poirot. Are you going to tell me what he is?'

'First why. The scarf is too new, too exactly tied. The ring is on the wrong hand. He is reading *Buddenbrooks* in the original language. In my view he is German, probably an actor, possibly homosexual.'

'You must have cheated!'

'Perhaps.' Max put down his cup. 'The café turc is sour. Well, I'll go below and spend a little time with Joseph.'

'I thought you'd nearly finished?'

'So I have but I can tell myself I have not. There is always another rabbinical gloss. The Yuya theory. The Arab and Persian stories. Even the Koran. An extraordinarily elusive figure still. I think I have caught him and then just as one feels one might pluck him by the sleeve, he turns away.'

Charlotte nodded. She thought of the faded photograph, Phoebe's violet-shaded face. Ghosts. Leo's artifacts. Niki's *Book of the Dead*.

'He was very beautiful, you know. That at least is beyond dispute.' Charlotte had noticed how Max's expression softened and changed whenever he was talking of Joseph. He spoke as one might of a son. He turned to Charlotte. That little smile. 'I will tell you the truth. I do not want to finish the book because when I have it will no longer be mine.'

'Do you have any family?' Charlotte asked. In spite of his courtesy and charm, one did not lightly interrogate Max.

'My dear parents dead long ago, of course. Oh yes, I was once fully equipped with family. I believe I have a few quarrelsome cousins left in Lithuania. That may be where I get my curiosity. The Litvak is always asking questions, never satisfied.'

'Children?'

'A son, David. He died on the Golan Heights. A reporter. Not a soldier.'

'I'm sorry.'

'Thank you. Well, I have been talking too much. You are a most sympathetic listener. No doubt I'll see you later.'

'I hope so.'

The sun was high. On the river the quality of the light was different, blindingly clear, no half-tones; by contrast the darkness was deeper.

When Charlotte woke Max was gone. The river had narrowed. In the distance she could make out a high stone bluff.

'Sorry. Did I wake you?'

'Niki. I wondered where you were.'

Charlotte shaded her eyes with her hand. He stood, back to the water, facing her, resting on the rail. The sweater had gone but the shirt was about as threadbare. All bones. The same air of a nervy bird about to take flight.

'Oh, doing courier things. You know. Thought you might like to borrow this.'

'Ah. Flaubert. Max Stiller was talking about it. Thanks. Yes, I'd like that. What courier things?'

'Just Hal's lot, thank God. Not the French. Pillows, light bulbs, general nursing. I don't think I'm very good at it. You?'

Charlotte yawned.

'I'm just being terribly lazy. Where are we?'

'Near Beni Hassan.'

'Oh yes, the rock tombs. What a pity. We'll have to land. What was that?'

'We bumped. Touched bottom. It's shallow here. Well. See you.'

'Sure to.'

Niki waved a hand and ducked away just as the lunch gong rang.

A small drama after lunch. Scuttering feet, shouts, an urgent knock on the cabin door.

'Aground,' Leo said. 'All on deck.'

'See how we all pull together,' said Max, sitting on an upturned beer crate.

Herded into the bows to lighten the stern weight, they watched as the pilot called to the crew who had jumped ashore with a line and to the boat pulling from the other

77

side. It was intensely hot and for most standing room. Only the honeymoon couple and a few of the French had failed to answer the call. Max was right, Charlotte thought. The modest threat from outside had for the moment broken down national barriers. When Marietta Southby pointed to the high bluff and said 'Bandit country', Italians, Americans, British and French exclaimed. There, indeed, ropes hung down from the cave openings that pierced the pinkish rock-face. Rumours were exchanged. This was a hideout for criminals. These were the entrances to ancient rock tombs. The story was that the season before last a party of Swedes on a small chartered cruise vessel had been attacked by night. Even if they got off, the engine would not start. The crew on the bank heaved and sweated and chattered and laughed. The two Australian girls leaped ashore to help. The *Hathor* shifted. Then she was aground again. Only the galabiya-clad pilot was solemn. Someone fainted. Hal boomed a running commentary. The pilot twitched the wheel tenderly with long, narrow brown fingers. He wore plastic flip-flop sandals. The honeymooners came up, holding hands, yawning. Then there was a cheer. They were off.

A flick of danger? Not even that, really. Only afterwards was there a feeling that for just an hour that afternoon they had been vulnerable. Under way again, the little *Hathor* became once more – so it seemed to the souls she carried – a small world complete in itself and in its completeness free of anything that might be happening beyond those dark banks.

At dinner Hal sat with Charlotte, Leo and Niki Yussoupov. Charlotte judged he had drunk just a little too much, hardly enough to show. She pushed aside the tough, unidentifiable meat and forked the potato.

'Where's Adila?'

'Working on tomorrow's lecture,' Hal said. 'Egyptian rites of death. This goddam food.'

'Nina said not to eat the salad. So did Marietta. But it's the only thing that looks attractive.'

'Nina says a lot about too much.'

'What happened at El Wasta, Hal?'

'Embassy wanted us to abort. Not for publication. Just another half-arsed attack of nerves. Fucking natives restless, as you Brits would say. Permanent situation, eh, Niki?'

'More or less.'

'It's OK, Charlie. Don't worry,' Hal said.

'I wasn't. I just wondered.' Charlotte smiled. 'There was a funny atmosphere in Cairo. But perhaps it's always like that?'

Leo and Niki were talking about mummification. After dinner Hal was quiet as the four sat waiting for coffee in the bar. He looked as though he had been punched. On the television a Clint Eastwood spaghetti western was being screened, dubbed in Arabic. The honeymooners were in a complacent time-zone of their own. Bed in their eyes. They would become unpopular. Marietta, the Australian girls and a small core of the British were playing Trivial Pursuit. One gang had formed.

Hal said suddenly: 'I tell you, Charlie, this whole country could go up. Any day. Any time. And you know what? I love the damn fools.'

Charlotte looked up from her book.

'D'you think Hal's really CIA? I mean, I thought they all wore button-down shirts and never drank. You know.'

'Double-bluff?'

'Mmn.'

'What are you reading?'

Charlotte looked at Leo. She saw them both, lying in their bunks in the small cabin, happy, the light on the blink, voyaging through the dark. She had rarely seen Leo so quietly happy.

'Flaubert. In Egypt.'

'Ah.'

Not that she was really reading. She opened the book at random. The whores of Cairo. The boredom of the temples she had yet to see. A comment on graffiti. Then:

'it is often as though I were suddenly coming upon old forgotten dreams.'

Black sheep, Joseph chicken. Travellers' names, which must have taken three days to carve. Ah, here it was: the yellow cow!

A deck below, Max searched irritably for a cross-reference (these sudden rages, he could never get used to them, spasms of temper, unfocused anger that signalled the assault of pain. Tonight he knew he had offended the waiter for no reason at all, pushing aside the congealed custard pudding, nearly slicing the dish from the table. Then stumbled from the dining-room in a cold sweat, vision blurred. (Doubtless the French thought I was drunk, clucked, passed judgment: *ivrogne*.)

The pain had at last tiptoed off, placated. Max settled more comfortably, pushed his spectacles up his nose and read. Yes, he had not been mistaken. Anthony, the first of the Desert Fathers, begs his disciples to save him from the Egyptian rites of the dead: 'Shelter in the ground, hide in the earth the body of your father.'

More of the same. Good. Max scented a footnote as he marked the passage, then turned to Genesis, from one deathbed to another nearly 2,000 years earlier, from Anthony to blind Jacob and the words Joseph heard. Max knew them so well he could close his eyes and with Joseph listen: 'bury me not, I pray thee, in Egypt: But I will lie with my fathers, and thou shalt carry me out of Egypt, and bury me in their burying-place.'

At least old Jacob had seventeen years with the son he thought never to see again.

Well, one dies, and does it really matter where?

If only David.

Ruth? Is that you? Take my hand. I can smell your hair.

Domed roofs announced that they were further south. The heat told them too. Minarets among the palms. In one

80

place they passed in mid-afternoon, the grass stretched out smoothly, like a mown lawn. And as Charlotte watched, tranced, from the shade of the narrow side-deck, an unseen muezzin called with unusual calm and gentleness, a drawn-out, lingering summons. The earth spoke.

5

'Here is life,' Adila told them, telling them what to see. 'Notice in the necropolis of Akhenaton no God but Aton, the sun, and many scenes of every day. Please shine your torches and you will see the dancing and the blind harping and the hair-dressing.' Her voice was that of a small, anxious, persistent bird. The acoustics of the rock-tombs played games with it. As Charlotte wandered away it flew after her. 'Akhenaton was the heretic Pharaoh who transferred his capital from Thebes. He is believed to have been a homosexual.' The bird disapproved.

At the mouth of the tomb Charlotte stood on the high bluff and saw, spread out, the great, empty plain they had crossed in the bumpy wagon drawn by a tractor. A waste of sand, the Nile shining silver beyond; people dotted about like actors on a stage. Even Marietta Southby, sitting on a stone bench, was silenced. Further along the escarpment Ed was filming. Leo had scrambled up the rocks above. Two figures – the honeymooners? – were planted out there on the sand. It was late afternoon and their shadows were long. Adila had switched to French. *'Ici on voit la vie quotidienne.'* Charlotte moved out of range.

There was a question here. Something to do with eternity. One blink of its golden eye and a daring kingdom swept away. Phoebe had come by donkey, a day's outing. 'Such sadness,' she had written.

Niki had said that death made life pointless. Up there in the direction Leo had gone was Akhenaton's empty tomb, sealed. When Charlotte's father was dying he was moved from the marital bed first to a divan in the dining-room, then to his study, the tiny hospital room, the coffin, as though, as death approached, the space he needed in the world diminished. So it did. The country solicitor who had never got to Egypt. The small boy who had received from his aunt sketches of life on the Nile ('Oops! Couldn't do it. Could you?'). *La vie quotidienne*. The soapstone Nefertiti on the brown-stained mantelshelf in his study, that Charlotte in childhood had always imagined to be a treasure of great value. One family Christmas she had found him in the study holding it cradled in his hands as he stood by the window that looked out on the wet, bereft winter garden. Howard put his finger to his lips as if imparting a secret. 'Hold it,' he said. 'It's warm.'

There was a shriek of laughter from Ethne, in the kitchen with her sisters, basting the turkey, a fag stuck to her lower lip, a g. and t. to hand.

When Howard was dying quietly, more fading than dying, Charlotte had wanted to ask him if he believed in life after death. She had suddenly wanted to ask this most urgently but she had been unable to frame the question (Ethne had trained her not to ask such questions). It was for his sake. His life struck her abruptly as so empty of anything (unless he had a secret: another secret more sustaining than dead letters and a passion for Egypt), it seemed desperately important that he should have at least the hope of something else.

Not that she knew anything about his life, when she thought about it, apart from the soapstone Nefertiti. She would have liked to believe that before Ethne, maybe with Ethne at first, he had had the dancing and the harping.

It struck Charlotte now, as the sun on the horizon blinked once, signalling the brief twilight and sudden night, that there were worse ways of going than Phoebe's: a brilliant life cut off by one slash across the throat. How much pain did one feel? How long would consciousness survive the gush of blood?

Then there was a clatter of stones and Leo was beside her.

'You've caught the sun,' Charlotte said.

'Have I?' He mopped his face with his handkerchief. 'Got any water?'

'Left it in the wagon. They're calling us now. Better go. Did you find Akhenaton?'

'Tombs sealed. Too far anyway. Most of them banked up with sand. Masoud said there have been finds. Rumours anyway. Archaeologists are pathologically secretive.' He was still panting. 'But I think I saw the Royal Wadi in the distance. Incredible.'

Such an effort, Charlotte thought, to catch what might have been a glimpse of an empty tomb. But then perhaps no stranger than her own search for a woman of no importance who died a long time ago.

'How did you get on?' Leo asked Charlotte.

'Adila explained everything twice in two languages. I liked the wall paintings. There's an extraordinary graffito on the ceiling of one of the chambers: W. Stephenson. He must have been an acrobat to do it.' Charlotte liked that. W. Stephenson.

When the wagon shook to a halt Leo said: 'Here. Look.'

'You're limping. Have you hurt yourself?'

'Nothing. I tripped. But look. Here, can you see?' A few stones in the sand. 'Nefertiti's palace. Not very big. There – there was a walled garden.'

Charlotte nodded. Here really was life – a trace of it, at least. Not a picture. Not a tomb. W. Stephenson. Nefertiti.

They were caught out by the sudden night. Crew-men came to help them between the bushes, across the ditch, back to the lights and the life of the *Hathor*. The children seemed to come from nowhere and ran after them all the way.

Life on the *Hathor* took shape. It was an illusion, of course, that this was a society complete in itself: a powerful fantasy, however, to those on board. Charlotte watched, amused. Hal had his drinking gang, Marietta her Trivial Pursuit party every evening in the bar. The travel writers, who rarely went ashore, had a poker school going (Leo did not join). The sun-lovers looked up and found the vessel too small. There was no top-deck for sunbathing. Even the deck outside the bar-lounge was half covered by an awning. The side-decks were too narrow for anything but a small seat pressed against the rail. Thus, a furiously selfish sub-dialogue broke out. As the voyage progressed the reins of what might be called civilisation – decency anyway – slackened. The greedily bold rose at six to put towels and books on the limited number of loungers facing the rail. The pretence that they had come on deck to catch the hallucinatory moment when Egypt appeared as the sun burned away the mist, grew fragile.

On this long stretch of the river where there was no landing Charlotte rested, tranced, against the side-deck rail. Sometimes she took her papers to a seat in the shade, sometimes to a table in the bar. As the voyage continued, Phoebe's story took on the feeling of a journey it would be impossible to abandon. The sense of contiguity was pleasing, sometimes startling. So that Charlotte would feel she need only shut her eyes and reach out and she might touch Phoebe's hand. One early morning there was a figure, surely, in the stern, about to turn and speak? Then the mist cleared and the deck was empty.

El Till, New Year's Day 1920

Dorothy, darling,

Got your letter just as we were leaving Cairo and expect this will reach you round about Easter if I post at Luxor. Do hope little Howard's over the measles and enjoyed my silly sketches and messages. Tell him I'd love it if he sent me something he had done and I have more for him. I think I miss him more than anyone.

Thought of him last night when we had a New Year's party and all the village children came down to the beach (girls enchanting – dressed in bright colours and full of life. Then they grow up and have to wear black and cover their faces not to be seen by us, the infidels). They were chased away from the boat, of course, but I got Amir to collect all our paper hats and he took them down with crackers and streamers and sweets and favours. So by the light of the boat there they all were, small brown figures running about in excitement and squealing and calling for more. We could hear them even when we'd gone to bed. Those are the sort of things I'll remember long after I've got in a muddle about tombs and temples – the children and the river.

I must tell you about something that happened just before we left (perhaps not Mother who'll say I'm keeping bad company). You know the Milner mission came out to investigate the March troubles? Well, my friend Nayra Hazim went with a lot of other women to demonstrate against it. If you knew this part of the world where the women are kept down so you'd understand these political protests are sensational. Much braver than our suffragettes. Nayra's such fun – when we're together we seem to spend most of the time laughing – but she's very serious about this, I think.

The sad thing is that I know there is a special bond between the Englishman and the Arab. Alex gets on wonderfully with the Egyptians. He treats them as equals and they respect him. He has a real interest in Muslim life and the Islamic religion . . .

'An incision was made in the left side. Lungs, stomach, liver and intestines were then removed and placed in the canopic jars. Through the nose the brain was taken out.'

Adila was telling them all about the ancient Egyptian rites of death. Her best attended lecture so far.

Life, death. Abydos, the temple to the dead. They came after a small drama, by calèches.

Charlotte listened, looked. Darkness thickening as one approached the innermost sanctuary. There was Leo, limping around. Happy. He was happy here. Note the goddess Nut, her arched body swallowing the light, giving birth to the morning. Yes, that was beautiful. But there was no life here. There never had been life here.

Phoebe must have seen the sparrows nesting in the temple

wall. Wagtails. Bees. The long, hot walk from the temple to the single tree. The yellow dogs with their pointed ears and dancing tiptoe walk. Marietta was feeding them the tough, dubious meat smuggled from last night's dinner.

Leo's secret life. All these years, good marriage, comradeship, passion, the small stuff that goes to make what is understood to be love; and yet Charlotte had never grasped until now how much he loved Egypt. (Howard and his soapstone Nerfertiti.)

Halfway to the tree, Niki loped up beside her.

Charlotte said: 'What was all that fuss about the calèches?'

'Money. You have to go to the top man and agree the payment. He was just being bloody-minded.'

'That's not all, is it? Why couldn't we land at Assiut? There was a horrible feeling going through the barrage. As if they hated us. The children didn't wave. Those stony faces.' They had spent the night at Assiut. The gang-plank was not lowered. Onshore Charlotte had seen a guard in a sentry-box. She had been reminded of the road-block in Cairo. And here. Something. 'Is it always like this?'

Niki shrugged.

'Don't pass it around but there've been riots in Cairo. This part's always strongly Fundamentalist. A European was shot in Assiut last week. You never know with the Egyptians. The Cairo business could be a coup on the way or the half-starved army's run out of shoelaces.'

Charlotte laughed. 'The thing about the Egyptians is. Poor Hal. He'd be heartbroken without Egypt. What about you?'

They were sitting under the tree, though even the shade was hot. Niki's thin hand, resting on his knee, was very white. The impulse she had had before returned: to take his hand in hers, to touch his face.

Then that quick smile and he stood up.

'Oh, me. I don't mind where I am.'

'Where were you before?'

They had reached the fence. On the other side the calèches were waiting, touts already shouting.

Niki said: 'British Council in Belgrade. Until I went on a binge with a visiting poet. Lost him. Taught English in Florence. Courier to the Costas. You know. Then Hobdoy's.'

'You've never been to Russia?'

'As a tripper, that's all.' Niki half-closed his eyes, recalling something. 'It's funny. I was always hearing about it at home, of course, but all I remember is Tolstoy. He was a sort of bogey-man of my childhood. My grandfather lived to ninety-five. He used to talk about him. Said he was a monster, a megalomaniac, a brute to Sonya. And Yasnaya Polyana was always cold. That was my childhood nightmare – that Tolstoy was coming to get me. Queer, isn't it? And I've always believed hell must be cold.'

'Then you believe in hell?'

They were sitting on a wall. The sun burned Charlotte's neck. She adjusted the scarf she wore under her sun-hat.

'I believe in Yasnaya Polyana.' Niki deflected the question. He kicked at a stone. Goats were chasing a dog over a rubbish heap. 'And yet, you know, I miss Russia – my grandfather's Russia. Maybe it's the Russian exile thing. Even the children are born dépaysés. Oh well, here are the others.'

At Dendera Charlotte stood with Leo in the dusk outside the temple of Hathor. 'Look,' he had said and then showed her the pylons marching across the Libyan desert.

'I'm beginning to see,' she said. They kissed. 'But I don't like talking about it. D'you know what I mean?'

The pylons struck her as right, extraordinarily beautiful.

There are rare moments when you feel you might, unexpectedly, have come upon a still centre.

Then Marietta's voice: 'Ed and I, our favourite goddess? Aphrodite as cow you know she suckled Horus and they slept together animal fetishism of course the nomad Dinkas of the Sudan? Midwife too? I think that's nice, don't you?'

That same evening one of the French girls came back on board in tears. She had been pestered by boys on bicycles on the dark, narrow road from the temple.

But it was nothing. A small incident. She was not hurt.

Increasingly as the river widened the *Hathor* became their real world. Going ashore, their bodies felt gravid, cumbersome burdens, as though they were spacemen stepping from one element to another. As the heat intensified the siesta was extended. Phoebe neglected her journal and there were few letters. Just a note of the first sight of the Theban hills and a sketch of Amir on his prayer-mat. Charlotte saw her, resting on a cane seat in the shade, a book unread on her lap, raising her face for Alex to kiss her.

Charlotte said: 'I've been having such dreams. But I can't remember them.'

Max nodded.

Nile dreams.

Max dreamed of his son. David brought him a toy to mend. Ruth came into the room and told him David was dead, it was time he went to sleep. Max was standing in a dark garden looking through bright windows into rooms (or perhaps it was all one room) where figures crossed the rectangles of light. And then they took their seats around a table, his mother at the head, David a young man now, next to her on her right, Ruth with her back to the window. Candled warmth. Laughter seen but not heard. A fabled aunt, who had been such a beauty, naked, fresh from the gas-chambers. A favourite cousin, the banker, tucking a damask napkin into his collar and spearing a dumpling. Max smelled the dumplings, rapped on the window and Ruth turned round and said: 'You can't come in. You're dead.'

Niki Yussoupov's vodka-dream: a narrowing tunnel with a black door at the end. Beyond? Tolstoy or nothing. Devil or oblivion. He woke thirsty.

Max looked at the temple of Luxor. They had tied up directly opposite, with only the corniche in between. Like old times, he said. Nowadays there were normally hotel boats stretching back for a couple of miles.

'Something to be said for a scare. Dreams. Yes. That's how Joseph got to the top – as an interpreter of dreams. Not in

89

the Freudian sense. More of a clairvoyant, I suppose. Magic – that still has a great appeal to the Egyptians.'

'Oh yes! Phoebe got her servant Saiza to take her to a wise man. A sheikh. It was meant to be a lark but he had some kind of epileptic fit. I wonder if he saw what was really going to happen.'

'How are you getting on with her?'

Charlotte thought. 'It's funny. In a way she's so close I can't see Egypt for her. That is, I'm not exactly seeing – I'm *recognising* Phoebe's Egypt, as if I'd dreamed it and I woke up and found the dream was real. Do you know that feeling? With Joseph?'

'Oh, yes.'

'I suppose one should come empty to Egypt.'

Max adjusted his spectacles.

'In that case one might find emptiness? Ah, I see Adila is calling up her chicks. Such as are left.'

The plague had hit the *Hathor*. Nile stomach, sunstroke, and after a strange day of wind, yellow cloud and a kind of sandy fog, there was an influenza-like virus. Marietta was worried about Ed's chest and had removed him for a couple of nights to the Winter Palace. Only Marietta could have found an American doctor.

'Death in Venice,' Leo said. 'The fatal khamsin. You're all right?'

'Fine. Just a touch of the sun. I should have known better. You carry on. I'll wait here. Or I might go back to the boat.'

'Sure?'

'Certain.'

'I love you.'

'I know.'

Since the sky had cleared, or perhaps because they were further south, the line between dark and light had sharpened; so Charlotte sat in the shade in the temple of Karnak and saw Leo limping away, reduced by both light and gigantism. Magnificent, of course. But the gods, if they had ever been here, were gone. And the kings and their mud-brick palaces. No life. Strutting Ramses and his boast. The dwarfs ran in and out, between the pillars. A babel of small voices in conflicting languages. Two parties met head-on. Adila had explained that only Egyptian guides were allowed onshore, so German and French became suddenly a scrap in Arabic, very fast, a matter of both status and ritual.

Yet there was something: the smile on the face of the Pharaoh, the complacency of power. Empire. Hal and his American fiefdoms. Phoebe and her love for the Egyptians? Was that in the end a sentimental attachment to a subject people? A reason for a death?

'A bit much, isn't it. Shall we run away?'

'Niki! Won't Adila be cross?'

They took a calèche – like a giant, brilliantly caparisoned pram on wheels, the driver on his precarious perch in one breath abusing the horse, yelling at the other drivers and the felucca-boys lounging on the corniche, and flinging over his shoulder remarks, questions and running commentary. Luxor Museum there. This afternoon he would come to their boat and take them to the Luxor Museum. Or the next day. They ask for him where they want to go. Mohammed – the name of the prophet – they remember? Easy! Very beautiful wife. How many childs?

Charlotte smiled, then laughed as Niki held up both hands: 'Ten.'

The driver rolled his eyes in admiration.

'Ten! Very good. English?'

'German,' Niki said, poker-faced. 'Deutscher.'

'Ah! German best in Egypt! Very good!' He whipped his bow-backed horse with even greater enthusiasm. The vehicle swayed alarmingly then swerved to cross the traffic, away from the river.

As they climbed the steps of the Old Winter Palace Charlotte was still laughing.

'Who'd win, d'you think? Mohammed or Marietta?'

Niki was watching her as they stepped into the garden.

'But this is wonderful! An English garden. Look – roses, hollyhocks. And a scent. Is it thyme?'

'I thought you might like it.' Niki ordered whisky for himself, lemon and Schweppes for Charlotte. She wondered vaguely if he were drinking as much as he had in Cairo. With the heat she had found she could not take alcohol at all in the day.

'We're being very naughty. Running away. Or I am, rather.'

'I kidnapped you.'

'Yes, you did.' There was something between them not spoken. Something Niki might say, must not say. Probably her imagination. It struck Charlotte that she had only seen despair close to twice in her life: here in Niki and in her father. Niki drank. Howard made up a country called Egypt. We all have our devices not to look straight at the pain of living. Leo and his artifacts. (Max? I believe he does look straight.) And why am I wasting Egypt in a pointless search for a woman who might as well have been dead a couple of thousand years? There are no degrees of death. No solar boat to carry us from the dark to the light. So why, now in this garden, and with Leo at Dendera, those queer unlooked-for glimpses of something quite small but eternal? Beneath the golden mask of Tutankhamun, behind Phoebe's dying eyes, in the silence of Akhetaton, in Howard's tidy English grave, the existence of the ka, the continuing spirit, seemed unlikely. Improbable. Yet possible? 'This is lovely. Thank you.'

'Won't Leo miss you?'

'He's going back to Gurna this afternoon. I'm afraid it'll be terribly hot. Some contact of Masoud's.'

'You're not? Did you enjoy it?'

'The Valley of the Kings? Oh, yes. Caught the sun there. Wonderful, terrible. That white heat. The touts. That awful rest-house. Then there was a falcon. Horus, I suppose. And someone held up a metal disc to show us how they got the light to do the tomb paintings. Like Plato's cave. Reflected sun and suddenly we could see the colours.

Brilliant.' Their glasses had been refilled. 'Where's Hal? I haven't seen him all day.'

Niki drank with precision, as if he measured out the whisky, dose by dose. After all there was an air of neglect. The high midday sun showed up the bald yellow patches the lawn-sprinklers had not reached.

'He's been trying to get the World Service since Assiut. Telephoning today, Cairo, London, Washington. Suppose I ought to be helping.'

Charlotte said: 'It seems peaceful enough here.'

Niki nodded. 'I say, d'you have to get back?'

'No. Nothing special to do. Hal and Adila asked round for me and I called at the American Express, the Post Office, the Bank, but if Phoebe's daughter is alive she's not in Luxor. Or she doesn't want to be found. Might be a chance at Aswan.'

'You very much want to find her?'

'Oh, yes. Very much. More than anything.' Charlotte considered the question. 'She wouldn't be old so she's probably alive. And Aswan seems the most likely place as she lived there as a child. In a way, I can't wait to get there. Then, it's silly, but I wonder if I really do want to find her. I did when I started on all this. Now I'm not sure. I can't explain.

'Of course, Pansy would only have been an infant when it happened. She wouldn't remember anything. Someone said Nina's gone straight to Aswan? But I've got a feeling she won't help me. She doesn't seem to approve. Anyway.'

They lunched and sat out the heat of the afternoon in the garden. Charlotte dozed and woke to find Niki watching her, pale eyes half closed. The shadows under the trees had grown darker. Someone (Niki?) had shifted the parasol to keep the sun from Charlotte's face. A small cat visited them. Charlotte was reminded of the beautiful mole-coloured Firdus and that other afternoon – which seemed very long ago – in Niki's chaotic flat. It was wonderfully peaceful in the English garden, as though this were a time out of mind and no harm could enter here.

'I wish we could stay.'

On the Corniche, even in the late afternoon, the sun stared and the touts no longer seemed picturesque. There was something alarming, aggressive, about them. Charlotte was glad to turn off into the souk, stirring from sleep, still not quite ready for business. Shutters were closed yet they were watched, she sensed, then decided it was imagination.

She might have been lost entirely but Niki was at home here.

'Illegal antiquities or souvenirs?'

'Souvenirs. Definitely.'

After the pungent and spicy odours of the street, the bazaar shop was cool. Niki haggled amiably.

'Smell them,' he said as he hung the long strings of beads over Charlotte's head.

'Sandalwood. Lovely.' Then a necklace of blue beads. 'You mustn't.'

'Don't worry. Not real. Nothing's real here.'

'But isn't that amber? And silver? Oh – look.' Rows of Nefertiti heads, quite well cut. Charlotte's exclamation had brought the manager sidling up. He wore a dark suit, slightly shiny, reminding her of Masoud's. 'Are they onyx?'

'They are very good.'

The manager beamed. He was inviting Charlotte to believe what she wished to believe. That was reasonable. A matter of connivance.

'My father had one of these.'

Niki was grinning like a dog.

'Soapstone.'

'I don't mind. I'll have one.' There were differences between them. They could not have been factory-made. 'This. Please.'

Outside, Charlotte smiled. 'You think I should have haggled?'

Niki shook his head, meaning, it didn't matter. He took her elbow and kissed her lightly on the cheek before they stepped out again into the sun.

'I'd like to see the temple again.'

There was something domestic about the Temple of Luxor that pleased Charlotte. The dust, the mosque in the wall behind the avenue of ram sphinxes; the impression Phoebe had noted in her journal: 'All in the middle of everything, built over, rescued, still seems as if the town might elbow it out.'

On their visit with Adila a couple of days ago Charlotte had overheard Marietta say: 'They've left a lot of dust over everything.'

There flitted past one of the shadowy Arabs, as ubiquitous in the temples here as the rock doves. Charlotte wandered away from Niki. The last exhausted crocodile of trippers was leaving. In the hypostyle hall she looked up where a dove called and could just make out the graffito, one name carved with splendid impudence: 'Rimbaud'. Rimbaud, W. Stephenson.

Glancing back she saw the neon sign on the dome of the mosque: *Allah*. Night had fallen since she entered the temple. By floodlight it was both more beautiful and faintly alarming. A sound like sandals. 'Niki?' she said and as she turned a stone struck her on the cheek. The figure in the galabiya paused between the pillars and was gone.

'Nothing. Truly. It doesn't hurt. Silly of me to go prowling on my own.' Charlotte remembered the looks of hatred at the Assiut barrage. She put her hand to her cheek. The stone had not even broken the skin. Yet she felt absurdly shaken. Spoiled was the word that came to her: something has been spoiled. Then an unexpected anger – not that she had been, in a small way, attacked, but that she had been given no chance to explain. As though she could have explained. (Had Phoebe felt that? Did the knife come out of the dark or did she see her assailant? Did she know him? Or even not knowing him, did she have time to say: you are wrong, you have made a mistake?)

There, a few steps across the corniche, were the lights of the *Hathor*.

Then Charlotte did laugh. Too sharply, there was an edge of hysteria, she heard herself laughing straight into Hal's face.

There he was, your drip-dry representative of American imperialism, poor old homeless Hal waiting for them on the gang-plank like a worried sheepdog.

'Where the hell have you been, Niki? The crew left an hour ago. They're not coming back. I've been running my tail off getting hotel rooms. State of emergency in Cairo. Get packed. Get out. It's no joke, Charlie.'

'No. No, I'm sorry Hal, of course it isn't.'

They had to step aside. Passengers were carrying their own luggage to a waiting coach. The fairy-lights were still strung between the trees.

Hal said: 'And where's Leo? Niki, do a head-count. Charlie, wasn't he with you?'

'No. He went back to the Valley of the Kings. Hal, what can we do?'

'I've left a message. Flying out in the morning. Fucking natives permitting.'

Hal was shouting across the crowded deck. Charlotte struggled against the press to get below. There was Max Stiller carrying a bag too heavy for him. Charlotte called but he did not hear.

By the time she got on deck again, the last to leave, something had happened. At first she could not make out what it was, then she realised that all the lights had gone out. Soldiers on horseback carried automatic rifles. It was not altogether clear if they were protecting or herding the *Hathor*'s passengers. An army truck drove past at a wild speed. Otherwise, the Corniche was eerily empty. The driver of the Eastmar coach seemed sullen and edgy. At the last dropping-point, a hotel near the station away from the river, he sat at the wheel and kept the engine running while the luggage was unloaded.

'So what's it all about?'

Charlotte had dug out her torch and, with the lift not working, found her way down to the candle-lit bar. Max, looking pale, was drinking mint tea. Hal was hunched morosely over his whisky. The small party had the air of refugees gathered

96

to await whatever would happen to them next. They were not exactly alarmed yet there was a need to be together: an artificial companionship but somehow a necessary one. Similar groups had formed among the others in the overcrowded hotel. The British were behaving with phlegm, the French with outrage.

Hal said: 'My guess, this goddam pan-Arab business. Nasser lives again. Libya's behind it, of course, and Iran behind Libya. Some Israeli high-up knocked off is the story.' He seemed to perk up slightly. 'Anyhow, Cairo's out. Not a seat on the only direct flight Luxor UK. So if we're lucky in the morning it's Alexandria or Aswan. And don't go out. There's a guard on the door and he's jumpy.'

'But Hal, that's ridiculous! I must find Leo. He'd hurt his leg. Anything could have happened. If he hasn't got the message. Where's Niki?'

'Checking out the airport.'

'But if it's dangerous?'

'Niki's part of the scenery. The original invisible man.'

'Yes, he is, isn't he.'

'Charlie, you always do me good. I don't know why. Can you tell me why you're the only woman for me?'

'Because you can't have me, Hal. And you're not half as drunk as you're pretending. So eat. Marietta's got us some sandwiches.'

'Charlie? It'll be all right about Leo.'

'Yes. Yes, I'm sure it will.'

The hotel was not quite seedy. That is, it was clean enough but the rooms were small, the beds hard and the service quite suddenly gone so they were alone as though on a ship which has lost its crew and in pitch-black night made a dubious landfall.

The Australian girls were sleeping on sofas in the bar. Hal was trying once more to telephone. Marietta and Ed had gone to bed.

'I suppose we should go too,' Charlotte said to Max. 'It's queer. I ought to be frightened but it feels unreal.'

Max smiled wearily. 'I think I shall go up. It probably is unreal, you know. By the morning nothing will have happened. That is Egypt for you, as Hal would probably say. Do you think they would mind if I took a candle to bed?'

'I'm sure they wouldn't.' Charlotte smiled. The little man, perched on a chair too high for him, looked even more like a frog than ever. She realised they were whispering as children do at night.

'I have found,' Max said, 'that it is remarkable how comfortable one can be in circumstances that appear quite terrible.' He spoke with gentle irony. 'Perhaps it is my race. So often we have had to make temporary homes in the dark corners of history. Not I myself, of course. Not that we have no reason to believe that history is up to her tricks tonight. So far as one can generalise about them at all, the Egyptians have an infinite capacity for adjusting reality. By the morning they may well tell you there is no emergency, the emergency never happened, it would be impolite to speak of an emergency.'

'I do hope you're right.'

In her room Charlotte sat on the bed, dozed and jerked with a shock from near-sleep. It seemed important to stay awake. She lit a cigarette, felt sick and stubbed it out. Digging in her bag she found the soapstone Nefertiti. She could hardly believe that only a few hours ago, this same day, she had been resting so peacefully in the garden of the Old Winter Palace, wondering vaguely if Niki Yussoupov had fallen in love with her.

She looked out at the square. In spite of the curfew a robed figure slept against the station wall. One of the dogs with the jackal-pointed ears was nosing through a heap of rubbish. As Max had implied, life going on regardless, the survival of the small and the ordinary. In the Theban necropolis there had been the miscarried foetus in the funerary temple. Charlotte remembered that and the falcon and the darkness and the light. The bright child-like pictures on the staring white houses of ships and planes: vessels that had carried the living souls to Mecca. As the ancients had visited the temple of death at Abydos. Necessary rites.

Then she did dream. Something about the open, empty graves in those indifferent, implacable hills. And she was falling and she would see if she wished to or not the bones that time and sand had washed. Howard? Leo? The children she had never had? A stranger who had disregarded the warning of the dragoman and wandered away? Herself?

There was a single crack of gunfire around midnight.

It must have been dawn because the candle had gone out and she could see him, when Hal tapped on the door.

'Leo's OK. Felucca boy brought a message from Gurna. He says carry on and he'll catch up. Niki's back. One flight to Aswan. Maybe Alexandria.'

Charlotte shut the door. In the middle of getting her luggage together she was suddenly caught out, knifed double by tears. Then, when she looked up and out of the window she saw that the sleeping figure had come to life. With the precision of habit he rolled up his prayer-mat. A woman, children and another man joined him and they appeared to be breakfasting. The woman was setting up a hubble-bubble. The smallest child was hugging the dog with the pointed ears. Sun filled the square.

In the house at Aswan Phoebe rises early on a November morning. The best time of day and the best time of year here after the summer's heat and before the khamsin. Pansy and Robin still sleep. She moves quietly so as not to disturb Amir or Saiza. Even after five years she is still amazed by the tropical luxuriance on one side and, across the river, the desert. The roses need watering. There were elephants here before the sand came.

Journal, Aswan, undated
Such peace here and the garden and the children. Miss Alex.
Learned not to ask what he's doing in Khartoum. Seems a
long time since we promised no secrets. It's the only thing that

separates us. Not so much his being away as not being able to imagine what he does in the Sudan. That is, I can see it roughly but can't picture exactly. And what dangers.

Know it's even hotter there yet see it as a dark place. The dark part of our life here, I don't know about.

Robin wakes even before Saiza. Love the children so much but need this time to myself before the day starts up. Am I getting a bit of a cabbage? Nayra's letters about the troubles in Cairo seem to come from a world away. Want so much to help and I *do* go about in the town and do what I can. Love it here and feel so safe, even with A. away. Amir such a treasure.

Funny. Half of me wants to be with Nayra and Ahmed, all those things we believed in. Believe. Then Robin comes in wanting to play from the moment he wakes up and I can hear Saiza talking to Pansy as if the baby could understand every word she said and that's all that's real. Ordinary things. Everyday. Here. The Nile. Life.

6

At the small airport information was unobtainable. Clearly, many had spent the night here. Besieged officials shrugged. Insolent boys in prickly ill-cut serge – tourist police – seemed no longer so much of a joke. There were other uniforms. Once inside the terminal, the would-be passengers were not allowed to leave. On the airstrip a small military aircraft shook in the desert heat. A big Danair jet took off for Heathrow. Rumours were exchanged. There was to be a special flight to London. Passengers must carry their own luggage. Everyone was to be strip-searched. The electronic security system had broken down. No flights to Cairo. A flight to Cairo at midnight. A plane landed but no one got off. It had come from Aswan. It had come from Cairo. The emergency was over. The emergency had never happened. Someone said Mubarak was under house arrest. There was martial law in Cairo. Risings in Assiut, Sohag and Balliana. One other civilian plane dozed on the tarmac. The Coca-Cola machine broke down. The boys in khaki serge attacked it with the butts of their rifles. They kicked it. An elderly German wearing Sony earphones announced that three European tourists had been slaughtered at Giza. Heads were wagged. But what had he said? Did he understand Arabic? Do you speak German? The French refused to share their mineral water. The fragile companionship of the *Hathor* did not survive the tension and the heat. It had never been quite real.

Charlotte sat on her suitcase. Niki was nowhere to be seen but Hal had come into his own. His finest hour. She saw him talking behind glass in an office. He thumped a desk with his fist. She saw him quite differently from this distance, in these circumstances. The certainty of being American, of power. What was he threatening them with? Nuclear missiles? The sixth Fleet? A withdrawal of the Coca-Cola concession?

Outside, the desert, its nothingness, its dispassion, put them all in their places.

Leo did not turn up. He had said, carry on.

'OK,' Hal said. 'That's it. Nothing to Cairo. Nothing to London. A few seats to Alexandria. Empty plane to Aswan. You've got to decide now, Charlie.'

Drip-dry Hal, Charlotte thought. It must be the combination of exhaustion, adrenalin, thirst and heat: whatever I say doesn't seem to matter very much. A miracle has taken place. Hal has conjured up an empty plane.

I could stay here and wait for Leo.

Then Pansy came into her mind, as if someone had beckoned. This might be the only chance in her life of finding Phoebe's daughter.

'Aswan,' she heard herself say.

Max pulled down his window-blind and closed his eyes. He argued quietly with the pain. A continuing conversation that might so easily have been ended in the airport lounge. No place to take one's final departure, on a hard plastic chair making another unseemly fall. So, given the chance, he had simply taken the first plane. The destination mattered less than the reason for leaving.

Hal was making his way down the aisle, counting his flock. Most, along with the rest of the *Hathor*'s passengers, had chosen to take their luck with the Alexandria plane. So far as Charlotte could see, there remained the Southbys, Max, Niki stretched out asleep across empty seats, Adila and the Australian girls from the other package.

'Don't worry about Leo, Charlie,' Hal said. 'I've left messages. He can take care of himself.'

Charlotte nodded. That had always been the understanding

102

between them. She could take care of herself. So could he. And yet there had been that sudden access of tears last night when she knew he was all right. In Egypt she had found herself aware, as never before, of mortality. Phoebe's story, perhaps. Time to digest Howard's recent death. Something to do with the light, the river, the desert.

The security man was coming out of the lavatory. No uniform, of course, but where his jacket was hitched up she could see the gun in his belt. He looked bored, heavy.

Below was the desert, shaped by the wind, in places smooth, then there would be wrinkles, waves, tracks that might be man-made or natural formations. Ed Southby, sitting behind her next to Marietta, leaned forward.

'All ocean once,' he said. 'You can still find fossils. The wadis – shaped by torrential streams.'

Sweet man. His eyes were bright. He smiled. Marietta nodded, patted his hand. She was proud of him.

Charlotte pressed her face against the small window. She looked down and saw Ed's sea, oceans of sand, eternity.

In her rooms above the bazaar Pansy Duncan shifted her complaining bulk. She could no longer bear the light. Sometimes she forgot her own name. Then things would be better for a while and on her two sticks she would make her way down to Fayoom's shop and sit at the back, listening, dozing, if she felt like it joining in the women's gossip.

Om Kabira they called her. Big mother. Perhaps she had helped them once. She could no longer remember, or only patchily, how she had become, how they had made her, the wise woman.

Pansy's vision had grown too milky to read them. Still, every so often she would take the key from around her neck, unlock the deed-box she kept under her bed, next to the chamber-pot, where the brindled dog slept and the kittens played, and feel the papers she knew by heart. She

103

would mouth the English words as a child might tell itself a familiar story to send itself to sleep when it lies alone and the light has been put out.

And Phoebe might almost be said to be waiting. That is, as Charlotte steps from the plane and the heat takes her breath away Phoebe is setting up house, waiting for her life in Aswan to begin.

In the winter of 1920 she does not yet know the names of the plants though she will learn later: lantana, hibiscus. She will cultivate a garden of her own on the island. Meanwhile she is excited, amused.

Elephantine Island, Aswan, 18th February, 1920
Darling Mother and Dorothy,
   At last! Moved out of the Cataract Hotel today and just enough sticks of furniture for us to sleep, live, eat. Cooks promise the rest from Heliopolis on the next steamer but am getting an old Egypt hand. Inshallah everything! Only way you can get by.
   Poor Amir very sniffy about this barbarian outpost (as he sees it). Such a Cairo-snob, you'd think they wore rings in their noses here. The people are handsome on the whole, darker skinned, tall, narrow heads, lively and friendly. Amir calls them monkeys. He had to recruit some to help with the move. You should see him as I can now – lording it over the work-crew, refusing to do a hand's turn while they are working though normally he'll take on anything. He's even got himself a dragoman's stick. Just hope he doesn't start beating them!
   Ah Sayidda, he says, wagging his head like an old woman, in summer such heat, we shall all be sick! A place fit only for camels. Just as if Cairo were London or Paris. Do hope he stops sulking soon.
   As for the house, it's almost the only one on the island. On high ground, verandah, rather like an outsize English summer-house. Lots to do to it. Someone lived here once because there's an overgrown tropical garden I intend to rescue (among many other good intentions). Saw it on our

honeymoon – wanted it at once. Alex let me have it though
I think he's a bit worried that he'll be away quite a lot and
I'll be stuck here on my own – though, of course, I won't
be on my own. Here's a rough plan of the rooms as they are
and how I mean to change them . . . When I told Rosemary
Gilchrist she said we were absolutely potty to live a) in
Aswan, b) on the island. Rather enjoy shocking R.G. Having
made up her mind we're bosom friends, she talks about
coming to see us as if we were one of Mrs Forbes's good
causes. Do hope Nayra comes though, as she promised.
Miss her terribly. She and Ahmed made such a difference to
our life in Cairo. Here's a snap of the four of us (Alex moved
so his face is blurred) in the garden at Heliopolis. Amir
took it so it's rather wobbly.

Must go. Some drama. Amir offended the Reis of the
boat bringing our stuff across the water. Shan't understand a
word they're saying but if I don't intervene my precious
book-crates will be dumped on the beach.

This will have to be a round-Robin for all the family.

Best love, and from Alex.

In haste – your incompetent, red-haired paleface from
the tribe of Woking —

Phoebe

Later that day, as Charlotte wakes from a sleep like
death in the air-conditioned garden suite on the island,
Phoebe cannot sleep. She walks through the rooms of
her house, imagining what they will be, plucks from the
darkness a vision of her garden, lights a candle and
sits with her journal for a while at the card-table. At
last she writes.

First night. Chaos. Envy Alex. After the Syrian campaign
he can sleep anywhere, just like an Arab. It will be all right
but more difficult than I've let them know at home. (Must
stop saying that. This is home. Shall make it home.)

Alex was all for sacking Amir but I have idea. Think
I'm pregnant. Hope I am. So I'll ask Amir, very seriously, to
send for a nursemaid from Cairo. Funny how if you stop
worrying about something the answer comes.

> Feel calmer for writing this rubbish. Will I really read
> it when I'm old and remember how I am now? Wonder
> – is there any such thing as the present? Or just the past and
> the future? I was very young in Cairo and maybe silly.
> And can't imagine being old. That might be why I'm writing –
> to catch this moment, the present. Must be midnight. While
> I'm writing that, tomorrow has become today.

Still groggy, Charlotte opened her terrace windows and stepped out onto the grass.

'We're summoned to Nina's but I put her off. Sit down, Charlie. Well, what d'you think of it?'

Hal looked as if he had been dry-cleaned. He was comfortable again in his skin. He too had a garden suite and was happy once more, his gang around him, a trolley of bottles, glasses, olives and roasted peanuts delivered by a racing waiter. He was happy. He wanted everyone to be happy.

Charlotte accepted a tall, cool glass. She had gone to sleep in the light and woken in the dark. For a second on the giant bed she had been alarmed, confused. Her hair was still curled and damp from the shower.

'Incredible. Weird. That crazy silver barge we came across on. All this. Surely these rooms were meant for more than one?'

'Rang Masoud from the airport. He fixed it.'

Charlotte shook her head. She let the evening wash around her. If there had been a faint air of unreality about the *Hathor*, this was a fantasy. The Southbys appeared. Marietta was saying she had already had a swim, it was the most wonderful pool but she'd been down to the health-club and there was nothing inside, when were they going to finish this place? You never knew with the Egyptians if they were going to finish or they were just letting it fall down and put your underclothes in the fridge dear, she had had the most fascinating talk about mummification with a real taxidermist in a Japanese group though it couldn't be Japanese, they'd chickened out, maybe I guess he was just small? Charlotte smiled. Niki sat on the floor by the window, sharp knees up to his chin. There was someone missing? Oh yes, Max. They made their way from the garden suites, past the pool to the Orangerie dining-room. Hal had recruited the Australian girls to his gang.

'Bizz and Fizz.'

'Sorry?' Charlotte forked at something ricey and fishy. Or was it chicken?

They both had burned noses they made no attempt to disguise. A disarming air of careless daring about them and vigorous curiosity.

'Elizabeth and Felicity. Awful, aren't they? So Bizz and Fizz. Have you been to Egypt before?'

'Oh, I see. No.'

'We're working our way round.'

'Round Egypt?'

'The world.'

'That's very enterprising.'

'Oh, it's not so big now, you know.'

The restaurant was almost empty but there was a crowd around the reception desk and in the travel office. Many looked dressed for a journey. Luggage was heaped in the foyer. Charlotte had meant to check on flights from Luxor.

In the large, low-ceilinged, dark bar Hal commandeered two sofas, deeply soft. Drinks all round. Charlotte left hers untouched.

'Is Max all right, d'you know, Hal?'

'Max is fine. You worry too much, Charlie. You're not worrying about Leo?'

'No.'

'Good girl.' Hal put an arm round her shoulders, then flung it up in greeting. Masoud had arrived. The Cairo suit had been exchanged for an equally immaculate outfit: white trousers and polo shirt, navy blazer.

'Welcome to Aswan.' He reached across the table to shake as many hands as he could. 'Nina sends her love. She expects you all tomorrow.'

He settled at the end of the sofa next to Charlotte. The waiters were immediately attentive. Too attentive? He would be known here, of course, but there was something else, a complicity.

Charlotte sat back. Hal was in great form, recounting some complicated story about an experience here with a film crew. 'I tell you, had to paint all the asshole camels. Too yellow, says this limey faggot. You ever tried to paint a camel? The thing about camels is . . .'

Marietta was delivering one of her monologues on the subject of travel precautions for the benefit of Bizz and Fizz, the low-down on Jerusalem. Niki was smiling vaguely. He had drunk a fair amount, Charlotte guessed, but as ever showed no sign of being drunk. His pale hair had fallen over his forehead. Charlotte wondered how soon she could politely go to bed.

'I'm sorry?'

Masoud was saying: 'I hope your husband found what he wanted in Gurna?'

'I don't know what he was looking for. Actually, I'm rather worried about him.'

'And why should you be worried?'

'Well, obviously. The emergency. Whatever it is that's going on.'

'There is no emergency, Missis Hamp.'

'Then why are there no flights to Cairo?'

'Now that I cannot answer. But I can assure you everything is normal in Aswan.'

'I'm glad to hear that. And now if you'll excuse me.'

'Walk you back?'

'Oh, Niki, hello. This ridiculous place. I've lost my way. I think I've just offended Masoud.'

'Shouldn't worry about that. There you are. The pool.'

'So it is.'

Niki seemed inclined to linger. He stood at the edge of the pool, hands in his pockets, his threadbare sweater thrown over his shoulders. There were lights on in the poolside duplexes. People were moving around in their temporary egg-box habitats, watching television, getting undressed. The dark water smelled cold.

'Planning a dip?' Charlotte said.

'Can't swim.'

Charlotte had been thinking. 'It doesn't make sense, but now we're actually here, I'm sure that Pansy is alive. Up to now she'd seemed like someone in a story. The only thing is, I don't know where to look. And I ought to wait till I know Leo's safe.'

Or was she just putting it off, she wondered? For fear of disappointment? Pansy might have nothing to tell her. And then if she had, Nina could be right, it might be something she did not wish to hear. Phoebe was so alive to her. She could leave it there.

They walked round the pool and down the steps to the garden suites. Charlotte unlocked her door.

'Well.'

'Can I come in?'

'Maybe better not. Don't you think?'

'I suppose.'

Niki seemed to take it lightly enough. He smiled, kissed her cheek and was off, head down. Shadow-man. Gone.

Now, Max wondered? The half grain of morphine? In London they had disapproved but if he absolutely refused treatment. Such a journey in his state of health. His responsibility. His risk. Finally it was an old friend who had equipped and explained his travelling pharmacopia. The morphine in particular, his last guns so to speak. Not to squander. He stood barefoot in the marbled bathroom, the glass of bottled water in one hand, the half-pill in the other. The crab was busy tonight, advancing on new fronts, Max suspected.

Silly old thing, Ruth said, death's nothing. She was sitting on the bed brushing her hair. It's dying you've got to watch out for.

*

109

Charlotte was beginning to get a sense of place. At dawn the river offered a precise, still picture of the desert, the tomb-entrances on the sandy hill opposite. A felucca was pinned to the water, waiting for a breeze. Outside her suite beneath the palms and the trees with the flame-coloured flowers, an elderly gardener worked. She looked away and when she looked back he was gone. There was a tall iron gate, by it an empty sentry-box. A girl with a red kerchief tied at the nape of her neck slipped between the trees carrying a heap of white towels. Charlotte felt no breeze but the felucca came to life, the sail filled, the picture was ruffled. Someone unlocked a padlock on the iron gate and exchanged words with the invisible gardener.

The refugees around the reception desk had begun to gather.

No, no message for Missis Hamp.

'Are there any flights from Luxor? Or a train?'

'You wish to go to Luxor?'

The clerk had whimsically decided to be helpful. He beamed at Charlotte as though indulging a small child. For as long as he cared to adopt an attitude of benign patience, the rest of the supplicants did not exist.

Charlotte said: 'No. My husband is in Luxor. I want to know if he can get here. Is there a flight?'

'Ah,' the clerk sighed. 'We have no information on that.' He brightened. 'A coach to Hurghada is possible. It may be there is a flight to Abu Simbel?'

'I don't want to go anywhere.'

This seemed to please the clerk.

'Then you have opportunities to visit the Island of Plants. There is also Philae and the High Dam. You wish a felucca?'

'No. No, I don't wish a felucca.'

'Philae is most beautiful. There is son et lumière.'

Charlotte gave up. There was a pantomime of disappointment. As Charlotte moved away the others surged

110

in to fill her place, waving tickets. The clerk held up his hand. He was weary again, afflicted by the responsibility of office.

In another part of the vast foyer, amazingly, Adila was concluding an address to her diminished party.

'At the granite quarry you will visit the unfinished obelisk. There will be opportunities for taking photographs before we proceed to the High Dam, completed in 1971.'

'Aren't you coming, dear?' Marietta asked Charlotte.

'I'd better stay around in case there's a message from Leo.'

'Well, the Dam's not so much really? A dam's a dam?'

'You've seen it before?'

'Oh, yes. We never miss the Dam?'

Hal was baking himself by the pool. He wore trunks, a peaked baseball cap, wrap-around sunglasses and a cardboard beak-shaped shield for his nose. He was timing his exposure and every so often turned himself. At the moment he was on his back.

'Hal.'

'Charlie. Hi. Going for a swim?'

'I went after breakfast.'

'Sit down.'

'Too hot for me here.'

Hal propped himself on one elbow.

'You're not still worried about Leo. He'll turn up.'

'Yes, I know he will.'

'Good girl, Charlie.'

In his spectacles Charlotte could see only her own face, reflected.

'All the same, I wish I knew what was going on.'

'That's Egypt for you.'

Max was resting in the shade on a lounger under a tree. He was asleep, breathing in little puffs through his mouth. Perhaps it was her imagination but he seemed thinner, his face had a waxy look.

Charlotte walked around the perimeter of the hotel. One block had the appearance of an airport control tower. It seemed to be empty. She saw the silver barge making its passage to the shore, the ugly, concrete buildings on the Corniche. Behind would be the bazaar, she supposed.

Tomorrow. Tomorrow she would look for Pansy. Perhaps. Perhaps Leo might come.

Phoebe sits on her verandah. Indoors the fan creaks. She writes at a card table.

23rd March, 1920

. . . I must tell you about this place. Here the desert comes
right down to the water, there is much less cultivation
than further north. And yet on Kitchener Island the most
wonderful flowers and plants. And here too my poor little
roses are having a fight to hold their own against the native
exotica – bougainvillea grows like a weed, there's no keeping
it back.

100 degrees today! Can you believe it? And it's only
March. I'll get used to it but at the moment it makes me
want to do nothing except perhaps write to you. Enclosed is
a rough map. You can see the island and our house. Below
us, beyond the garden, the beach where there are supposed
to be all kinds of things to interest an archaeologist. All
I can find is a lot of shards and a few stones that might have
been part of a temple. Alex often goes down there and
pokes about. In Cairo he ploughed right through Denon's
Déscription de l'Egypte. Too much for me. All the same
it's queer to think of Napoleon's army and how amazing
it must have been for Denon when Egypt had been closed to
the rest of the world for so long. You know in Luxor
Temple the French army formed ranks and presented arms
without being ordered, in honour of the dead Pharaohs.

Amir settled down, thank Allah. Almost his old cheerful
self. Got him to send for a maid and she arrived from Giza –
his cousin, or niece or sister's cousin, not sure which. Saiza

112

– a sweet girl. She's out there now spreading the washing to
dry on what we call the lawn. Anyway it's cheered him up.

Tell Howard I've got him a present I think he'll like
for his birthday, since he's clearly an Egypt-scholar, or going
to be. I'm putting a little story with it & will entrust only
to the safest hands . . . Nayra if she comes or Alex when he
next goes to Cairo.

You can see from the map we look south. In fact, we're at
the end of Egypt here. Nubia and the Sudan beyond, where
A. is now. Yes, please, send me the nasturtium seeds. And
if it's not a nuisance, Maugham's *The Moon and Sixpence*.

Love to all and a special hug for Howard.

Journal

Haven't told them at home about being pregnant. Mother
will only panic and try to get me back to England. Letter
from Nayra. Sounds as if she really might come. Says she's
lots to tell me about the Wafd (troubles?) but will wait till
she sees me or can send letter by someone she trusts. Does
this mean they're opening mail? Seemed a bit down, cryptic
anyway. Enclosed nice message from Ahmed. Evening.
Miss A. quite badly this time of day. Just for half a minute
almost wished still in Heliopolis with Rosemary G. Someone,
anyone, to distract me. Only my 'interesting' condition
making me think silly thoughts. And a change in the weather,
cloud, colder, sort of sandy fog. Khamsin coming, Amir
announces and in a lordly way gets our Nubian to go round
the house closing all the shutters. Saiza laughs at him and he
doesn't like that at all. But cheers me up. Tomorrow giving
her another English lesson. 'Tomorrow!' she says in her
funny accent, as if tomorrow were a special secret between
us. *Demain* says Saiza (French comes more easily to
her). *Bukra* I answer. Wonder if that's right, if I'll ever be
able to carry on half a sensible conversation in Arabic.
Tomorrow . . .

'Oh, my poor darling children!'

Nina Fahmi threw up her hands. She was wearing a white
silk sheath that stopped above the knees and getting away
with it. Tiny, pointed ivory-coloured shoes.

113

Most had ridden by calèche from the road above the Oberoi landing up and away from the Corniche, past gardens, greenery, hotels, to Nina's bungalow. Outside, high white walls and an iron gate; within, a tidy garden, much of it paved.

Max had preferred a taxi to an unsprung calèche and Charlotte had shared it with him.

'You've been here before? To Nina's, I mean?'

'Yes.' He grinned as Nina came out to meet them. 'Worthing Moroccan, I always think. Amazing what a difference climate makes. Nina, my dear, you look wonderful.'

'What you have all been through!' Nina exclaimed. She drew them indoors. It was already dark though tonight there was no chill in the air. 'First that frightful river and then such a scare. Those terrible people – when I think what they might have done to you!'

Max raised his eyebrows.

'You know more than we do, Nina. Who are these terrible people?'

'The Egyptians, of course! Oh, you're teasing me again.' Another squeal and she was off to greet new arrivals. A servant appeared with a tray. Charlotte took champagne, Max whisky.

Max led the way to a quieter spot, a chintz-covered sofa, flanked by two tall figurines, blackamoors bearing electric flambeaux. Not quite Worthing, after all. With Hal's appearance the party had really begun. Watching him embrace Nina and whirl her around, Charlotte understood: he's happy now – or a degree less unhappy. Off the river. The river frightened him.

Max was saying: 'Nina likes to think of herself as an exile. Doubtless you have noticed. Yet without Egypt she'd be lost. Well, Aswan is a great place for exiles. Poor old Juvenal sweating it out at the southernmost border of the Roman empire. The Jewish frontier guard on Elephantine. The conscripts at the High Dam now. One can imagine.'

Charlotte thought he had forgotten her then suddenly

114

Max concluded: 'You must see the graffiti at Philae. They have moved the temples, I know, but the inscriptions remain. There one can see it. How terrible it was to be in such an unforgiving land, so far from home.' His tone was mild.

'Exile?' Charlotte tasted the word. Niki Yussoupov was in her mind, and Hal; and her own father self-condemned to some kind of lifelong exile from a country he had never visited. His aunt invented it for him perhaps, the Egypt of the letters. He never got over it. There was some more precise proposition but Charlotte could not quite catch it, pin it down. 'D'you think Joseph felt like that? Exiled?'

Max raised his spectacles and rubbed the bridge of his nose.

'I used to wonder about that myself, a great deal. It is in the Jewish nature, of course, although historically we have been more contented and useful exiles than we have been given credit for. Frequently we enriched the society in which we found ourselves. On the other hand, yes, always the longing for the dreamed-of homeland.'

That little flash of irony, the corners of his mouth turned down.

'Do you feel that? Have you felt it?'

With a clean handkerchief Max was rubbing the lenses of his spectacles. Without them he really was a mole. Purblind. Not a man who relished interrogation, he might well deflect her question.

'I consider myself to have two nationalities. I am English and I am a Jew – though lapsed, as the Catholics would say. Israel – in the early days I knew the fervour. I have reasons now for hoping to visit Jerusalem. But it is no longer a place I could live. A sadly tarnished Utopia, I fear.' Max replaced his spectacles. 'As for Joseph, you must remember he was very young, ambitious.' Max's tone was livelier, he was onto his favourite subject. 'Egypt was his America, his new-found land. He seized every possibility. He got to the top. Far too busy to worry about exile. But I must get off my hobby-horse. How is yours?'

'Oh, Phoebe,' Charlotte said. 'I'm beginning to feel closer, if you know what I mean. Nothing concrete though. Maybe I've been very unprofessional about the whole thing. I can't detach myself enough. I've read and re-read the material. It's funny. Part of me's worried to death about Leo. And yet I can't stop thinking about Phoebe. As if she were real – alive, I mean. A sort of necrophilia I suppose, to be so obsessed by the dead. Anyway, what I need most is to find Pansy Duncan – the daughter – if she's alive. I think Nina might know something but she's not telling.'

Max smiled and nodded.

'Nina has an infinite capacity for not looking at anything that might be unpleasant. She even managed to ignore the war – quite an achievement, living in Cairo. Or rather, she simply went on being Nina.'

'You are talking about me.'

'Everything nice, my dear.' Max looked up. Nina perched on the sofa beside him and patted his knee. Max continued to smile. 'And now you are going to be nice enough to tell Charlotte anything you know about Pansy Duncan.'

There was a shout from the other side of the room. Hal with his arm around Adila's waist. Was it Niki arrived?

'The Duncan woman?' Nina said. 'I know nothing about her at all, nothing of any use. There was talk years ago about a European gone native but I never met her. No doubt she is dead. Now, come on Charlotte, Max cannot keep the pretty ladies to himself.'

Partway across the room, Nina paused, but did not relax her surprisingly strong grip on Charlotte's elbow.

'I expect that Max will have told you that I pretend the horrid things are not there. This is not true. I see them very well but I do not invite them to dinner. What is the point? All they will do is eat up one's happiness, these spoilers. This is why I tell you not to look too deep.' Nina did not wait for a reply. 'Now please, tonight enjoy yourself.'

It was hard, as ever, to tell if Niki was drunk. Certainly there was something about his mood: his eyes were bright, he looked as if he might have a fever. He smiled at Charlotte and raised his glass as she went to stand beside him.

Hal was holding forth to Bizz and Fizz and anyone else who would listen.

'I tell you, while the States pay the bills they can't sell out on Camp David.' His sombre mood had lifted entirely since they arrived in Aswan. Another one, thought Charlotte, who sees what he wants to see. Maybe, unlike Nina, he doesn't always succeed. He has more to lose: Egypt.

Ed Southby tapped the bowl of the pipe he never lit.

'But Hal. The business in the occupied territories. It's not just the Gulf any more. And it seems to me, don't we have to take this Pan-Arab rising seriously?' Ed's tone was quiet, thoughtful, as though laying before them an academic proposition. Charlotte could see him, a popular teacher before his class of keen young agronomists. Perhaps a lifetime of greening the earth gave one a sharper and sadder perspective upon the folly of human politics. When Ed dreamed, it was of an harmonious planet, nature in accord with itself, man its husband and helpmeet.

'Mubarak'll crack down on that.' For once Hal sounded less than convinced, then he downed his Scotch and recovered himself. 'The thing about the Egyptians is, they can play it all ways at once and make every game look for real. Virgin tarts. No offence, Adila. Don't get me wrong. Anyone who can screw the Russians and the Yanks. Love 'em all. Nina! Will you get this damned monkey off me?'

'Tottie, come here at once.' Nina called Masoud. 'Masoud! Hal is frightened of poor little Tottie, who wishes only to kiss him.'

Charlotte laughed.

'Whatever is it?' she asked Niki. The animal had limbs like a furry spider. It was attempting to groom Hal.

'Nina's lemur. She keeps it here at Aswan. To annoy, I think. Masoud hates it. I say, d'you want to stay here particularly?'

'Not especially. Why?'

'Got a surprise for you.'

'Have you?'

'Let's go down the road first, though. Before the others get the same idea.'

'Where've you been anyway?' Charlotte asked. They strolled down through soft, warm pads of darkness and then were walking between floodlit flower-beds.

'Hold on,' Niki said. He led the way into the nearly empty marbled hotel foyer and out to a covered terrace. Two sides were open to the air. Large insects beat themselves against the light; beyond, there was a falling view of pink granite down to the river.

The high ceiling, shabby tables and chairs – few occupied – a tall, dark-faced Nubian yawning in a corner, the general air of splendour decayed, presented the illusion of a stage set from which the actors have long departed, the drama done.

The waiter flip-flopped across to them, his plastic sandals incongruous beneath the galabiya. Niki ordered cognac and Turkish coffee.

'Well, what d'you make of the Old Cataract? Gone downhill, I'm afraid, along with the Turkish coffee, if it ever arrives. Ah, the cognac. Rather like it myself. Bit of faded Empire.'

'Phoebe stayed here.'

'Yes? That would be the grand days.'

'Is this the surprise?'

'Oh, no.' Niki downed his brandy and signalled to the waiter. Charlotte felt sure that he had drunk a great deal even before he had arrived at the party, though the only sign he gave was the need to keep on drinking. 'No, I've been fishing for you, followed up some talk I'd heard before about a Sayidda Shaikh living in the bazaar. A wise woman.

118

I knew she was a European. I'm pretty certain now it's Pansy Duncan.'

'Pansy! Alive? But that's wonderful. Have you got the address?'

'I can take you there. Though she's ill and a bit of a hermit.'

'Thank you. I'm really grateful.'

'Tomorrow then? Or the day after. When I can fix it?'

'Tomorrow. Fine. Whenever.'

The coffee when it came was thin, grounds floating on the top. After all, the party did not follow them. The other tables emptied.

'What will you do,' Charlotte asked, 'when this is finished? Back to Hobdoy's?'

'Might go on south.' Niki shrugged. 'Your Phoebe. You said once she broke the rules? Was that why she was murdered?'

At their backs the waiter flapped away invisible dust from the tables. The dim lights flickered. The true stage was below: the Nile, the desert, the island. Phoebe's house would have been down there somewhere, at the southernmost tip of the island. There was a Nubian village now, someone said, through the gate from the ridiculous hotel; a museum where Phoebe's house was.

In the dark; in this cockpit above urgencies, above everything, talk was easier. The twin glow of their cigarettes was companionable.

'No. Though that would explain the newspaper report, why Phoebe is almost passed over although she was the victim. I've been thinking about that a lot. Clearly she got involved with the independence movement – the Wafd – at least, she supported her friends, Nayra and Ahmed Hazim. I'm not sure to what degree because there are some pages of the journal that seem to be missing. That would make her unpopular, a pariah as far as the British community was concerned. So it would be the most awful irony if she were murdered because of the anti-British feeling. But what other reason could there have been? I don't even know where she was buried. If she was buried.'

'What about the husband?'

'Alex. My father told me that after the murder he asked for a posting in India. He went rather odd, I think. The family lost touch with him completely. He took Pansy with him. Died of cholera early in the war, when Pansy was about eighteen. She refused to leave India, stayed with an English family and after the war seemed to disappear. There was just this story that she'd come back to Egypt. Then nothing.' She was aware of Niki watching her. 'Sorry. I can be a bore on this subject. Shouldn't we be going before we're thrown out?'

Across the road there were signs of life and light from the souk but the Corniche was dark. Light and dark. Life and death. Over the river on the sandy bluff the floodlit tombs of the nobles, on the sky-line the domed shrine of a forgotten chief.

Niki's warm arm brushed hers.

Charlotte said suddenly: 'It was terrible, my father's funeral. Damp. English. Gabbled through. Then an awful sort of cocktail party with my mother as heroine. They do it better here, don't they? Wailing in the streets? And the Jews and the Irish.' She walked on, hearing her own voice. While she talked she was thinking, there is some connection; looking for the truth about Phoebe's death perhaps I am grieving for Howard. And Phoebe – what ceremony did she have, the Englishwoman with an inconvenient passion for the Egyptians? Of course Leo was all right, but if anything were to happen to him. 'I think there are necessary rites. And we neglect them.'

Adila had told her when, in modern times, archaeologists took Pharaohs in their pathetic wrappings from a rock cleft downriver to Cairo, the countrywomen wailed for their dead kings departing.

Then there was the tinkle and clop of a calèche behind

them and Niki was suddenly in the middle of the road, very drunk, his hands cupped, yelling at the black sky.

'Come and get me, Tolstoy, Lev Nikolayevich, you old bugger! I know you're there! I hate death! Hey, where are you then, shit-death?'

'Niki, for God's sake.'

Hal jumped from the calèche and for a moment he and Niki seemed to be fighting in the road, then Niki sagged against him.

Sometime around two in the morning Charlotte wakes from a dream she cannot recall. From habit, she reaches for Leo. She remembers Niki, the sight of him standing in the road, flinging up his arms after his imprecation, the calèche driver reining in his horse just in time. Her own feeling of helplessness and shock while Hal supported him on one side, Bizz or Fizz on the other. 'Not your fault, Charlie,' Hal had called across his shoulder. Charlotte had felt ashamed all the same, as though she should have known, stopped Niki drinking. Gone to bed with him? Not talked about death? Coaxed him back to life, into life?

Charlotte shakes her head. For the second time that night her father comes into her mind. In dying, he has grown younger for her. He is the child, standing in a holiday photograph on an English beach, imagining Egypt. In the sand he builds not castles but pyramids, gravely, alone. Someone calls. He looks up.

Phoebe looks up, smiles, ponders, then writes:

Aswan, April 1920

Darling Howard,

Uncle Alex is just leaving for Cairo so I am giving him this Egyptian princess for you (her head anyway) to make sure it gets safely on the next ship.

Her name is NEFERTITI. She lived over a thousand years ago by the Nile and was the beautiful wife of a famous Pharaoh who worshipped the sun. Nefertiti had six daughters. All through her palace there were lovely wall pictures – even the ceilings were painted, with water-birds flying.

The end of the story of Nefertiti and Akhenaton is sad but while they lived they were very happy. Akhenaton wrote poetry and Nefertiti played in a walled garden with her six daughters.

And you find that very boring, I expect, and would much rather know that Amir was stepping into the felucca the other day and fell in the water! All the local boys swim here and the women use the water for their cooking and washing. But Amir believes everything in Cairo is good and everything in Aswan is bad – including the Nile. He made such a fuss and got even crosser when the felucca boy laughed at him. He was quite sure he was poisoned and lay on his bed groaning and moaning and holding his tummy. Saiza couldn't do anything with him. He was raving that he had a big worm inside him and would die of it when it ate him up. Only got better when Uncle Alex pretended to be very stern and serious and gave him a big dose of castor oil. You can guess what happened next! Anyway, it worked, and Amir is back about his duties but expecting a lot of sympathy and very self-important. He says – wagging his head – he is a man snatched back from the brink of death. Here is a sketch I did for you of Amir falling in the water. Had to make sure he didn't see it. TOP SECRET.

So you are off to prep school in September! Darling, no of course I won't tell your mother anything you write to me, if you don't wish me to. It's *quite* all right not to want to go. What a pity they don't take dogs as well as boys. But truly, Teddy won't forget you and it will make the holidays even better to be with him again.

I don't think it will be as horrid as you expect though it will take a bit of time to get used to it. What I want you to do is promise you will write to me and tell me everything you want to as often as you can, even if it's only a short note.

Ramadan here now, which means Amir and Saiza can have nothing to eat until the sun goes down. I have to be very careful what I say to Amir, when he is starving! But he's

a good soul. He knows all about you (I have your photograph
on my desk) and says he will pray for you. So does Saiza
who longs for you to come here – she even kissed your
picture. You will be the only boy going to Stoddards under
the protection of Allah.

Even with Uncle Alex taking this to Cairo I expect it
will be ages before you get it. In time for your birthday
in August, I hope! You'll be at Bembridge then, having a
wonderful holiday, I'm sure. See if you can build a pyramid in
the sand and ask mother to take a photograph for me.

Have a very happy birthday, darling.

With my very best love – and salaams from Uncle Alex,
Amir and Saiza,

Aunt Phoebe

At four in the morning Charlotte gives up hope of sleep.
Twice she calls the desk clerk. Once there is no answer.
The second time a sleepy voice: no message. She pours a
glass of Perrier, turns on the desk lamp, lights a cigarette.
Room here at last to spread her papers. Knowing the words
almost by heart, she listens now, rather than reads. Senses
tensions between the lines. The clear voice of the girl who
came to Egypt is modulated, growing more thoughtful, less
impulsive; tending always to hope, looking for the best
of things while acknowledging, privately at least, in the
journals, that this life she has so guilelessly undertaken
will not be easy. Charlotte listens.

Cairo, June 12th, 1920

Dearest Mother,
You should see me now sitting in the Gilchrists' garden
in the shade, with my feet up, a bell to hand in case I should
urgently require a handkerchief or a cup of tea (English,
of course – nothing but Jackson's best!). I am hardly allowed
to put my feet to the ground and shall soon be sent indoors.
Feel like a woman in a harem, permitted to do nothing
but eat and make herself pretty, neither of which appeal to
me in my present state. I tell Rosemary I am not dying
of consumption, simply pregnant which is a natural condition

123

not an illness but she is so kind and fierce, you could not do better yourself.

It would have been quite absurd for you to come out (though bless you for the thought). Such a long journey and when you got here there would be nothing you could do. I have Saiza and Rosemary's servants and Alex will be here next month. And I have the best *English* doctor.

As for taking the baby home to Aswan, I am quite firm on that, Mother, so please let's not write about it any more or we shall quarrel. Yes, of course, there are illnesses among the fellahin but no more in Aswan than anywhere else. And I'm not planning to bring up him/her in a mud-brick village or a bazaar. We already take every precaution and if we need to we can isolate ourselves entirely on the island.

A treat yesterday. My Egyptian friend, Nayra Hazim, had managed to get a copy of Colette's *Chéri* from a Frenchwoman who hadn't even cut the pages. I'm stumbling through somehow, wishing my French were better and missing every other word. But such fun. Just right for my mood . . .

Journal, June 1920, chez Gilchrists

If only Alex had agreed that I could stay with Saiza in an hotel! Shall go mad with boredom long before the baby arrives. It was awful to part from Alex on bad terms. Lovely letters from him since. But why couldn't he see my point of view? Since we left Heliopolis something's hardened in my mind and am unable to find any common ground with Rosemary at all . . . entirely out of sympathy with the Gilchrists and everything they stand for. Their assumption that what they do for Egypt is right for Egypt. By the time she's forty Rosemary will be just like Mrs Forbes . . . Not being fair, I know. R's attitude normal, mine peculiar. It's the tribe. Rosemary just goes along with the customs. Alex too, I suppose? But he *is* different? Really loves the Arabs, treats them with respect. If it came to the crunch though, wonder what he'd do.

Nayra here yesterday when Rosemary was out. Such a relief to have a proper talk, not about bridge, servants and

124

correct conduct for heavily pregnant English Sitt – as the men call us. (Not Alex!) N. says everyone waiting to see what Zaghlul will achieve with London negotiations. Not much she thinks, given attitude of British government.

She told me all about women's demonstrations against Milner mission at the end of last year. Begin to understand the female Wafd remarkable – to have broken out of the harem brave enough to begin with. This is revolution for women as well as for Egypt. They have support from foreign women – quite a few French. N. frank about brutal behaviour of our soldiers. If only I could help! Never thought I'd be ashamed of being English . . . Nayra such fun too. Not just politics talk. Messages from Ahmed.

Talk of the town is Lebanese girl who has married rich Coptic Christian, buys her frocks in Paris, her knickers in London and throws parties regarded by Egyptians *and* English as terribly shocking, which means must be frightful scandal among the Copts – her poor husband. Rosemary came in just then (thank heaven not half an hour earlier) and said Mrs Forbes has declared Nina Fahmi *persona* definitely *non grata*. R. is human after all. Admitted she was dying to meet Madame Fahmi if only to find out what's so shocking about her . . . Then spoiled it that evening by warning me off the Hazims. Cairo Police Department have Ahmed on their blacklist, Nayra a very sweet girl who has been misled. Geoffrey Gilchrist says this is time we may all have to stand up and be counted, close ranks, possible embarrassment to Alex, etc., etc. . . . Pretended to take myself as warned. Writing this now to let off steam. Then indigestion and baby kicks. Feel like some enormous fruit that's going to burst. Can't sleep. Saiza sits with me. Beautiful night. She's so sweet and longing for the baby – such a calming presence.

Max awakes. For once not sweating. Clear-headed. A kind dream is still upon him and he reaches into the bedside drawer for his wallet, the photograph of Ruth and David, holding hands, both squinting at the sun. This sense of the vitality of the dead – nothing more, he supposes, than a self-willed illusion. He has seen it before among

125

the old and the sick. Well, anything to ease the leaving of the world.

Which apparently is not to take place today. The crab is napping. A remission. He feels better, even a little hungry. He is back in the present, looking forward to today.

Charlotte flicks through the papers and, without knowing what she is looking for, makes her own notes on a fresh pad.

August in Cairo, 1920. Robin is born. The Duncans take a house for six weeks before undertaking the journey home to Aswan. Phoebe is busy and happy with motherhood. Letters home are short and reassuring. Firm and placatory towards her mother who has clearly demanded her return to England. Funny little notes to Howard about his new cousin.

> By the time you come to see us in Egypt he will have
> stopped bawling for his food and be eating his dinner with
> a knife and fork. At the moment he would bore you to
> death since he cannot hold a conversation at all. He is
> very precious to me but then mothers are stupid, dreamy
> creatures who talk Ug-language perfectly happily for hours
> on end. Saiza too is fluent in Ug, with an Arabic accent.

Nayra gives Robin a beautiful edition of the Koran, with a hand-tooled leather binding, and a silver bell.

At the beginning of October the family return to Aswan.

From here on, Charlotte is aware that Phoebe speaks with two voices, one for the letters, the other the journal – though there is some overlap between the two.

> *Journal, December 31st, 1920, Aswan*
> Robin's first Christmas! Two Christmases, since we cele-
> brate January 7th with Coptic friends. New cook served
> fierce-looking Nile fish none of us could eat but made up for
> it with wild turkey – bit tough but spicy flavour. Amir
> helped me dress a palm branch for tree. Informed me loftily
> that it was the angel Gabriel who announced the birth of the
> prophet Mohammed and that Jesus was not a bad chap at all

126

– or something to that effect. Quoted the Koran. Looked it up in our translation and there it was! Surah 19 – poor Mary having awful labour under palm tree. Lots of other mentions. Must ask Alex more about it.

Nayra's letter says terms for independence the Wafdist leaders brought back from London last October completely unacceptable. Men *totally* disregarding the women's sacrifices and efforts and tried to hide terms from them! Not Ahmed, of course, but he's a lone voice . . . Wish I knew him better. From our first meeting he has struck me as an Egyptian I could *really* talk to, without that male superiority thing so many of the men affect.

Feel there will be terrible bloodshed if things go on like this. Alex doesn't seem to want to talk about it (came back exhausted from the Sudan and not too well). Because there's no one else to talk to except Nayra in letters, am so muddled in my mind. When I first talked to the Hazims it seemed so clear and simple – a matter of plain justice. Much more complicated now, since having Robin and running busy household etc. If things get worse we are all in danger. Which means those I have such sympathy with are the very agents who might threaten those dearest to me. However indirectly. So here I am, a member of the 'tribe'!

Love this place so much. That helps. Desert and river always. Make human problems so small and absurd. Life like the Nile? Long smooth stretches of time then cataracts, rush, muddle, until it settles again and flows broad and wide.

Elephantine, April 30th, 1921

. . . So, Dorothy, please persuade Mother that Robin will *not* be eaten by a jackal or anything else. Nor will he get malaria, yellow fever, cholera, typhoid, the black death or anything worse than mild heat rash as he has our awful family gingery colouring. Can't promise not measles but what with Saiza, Amir, myself, our Nubian, the washerwoman, cook, myself and all his doting admirers, he is the most spoiled baby ever. Seriously, I really cannot keep up this fuss with Mother. If she writes in that tone again I'm not sure I can bring myself to reply. Sorry you're pig-in-the-middle, bless you.

127

With Alex away even more, have become a demonic gardener, out in my sunhat all hours. Saiza clucks at my leather skin and freckles but have actually managed a good vegetable plot. And persuaded our Nubian (in no common language) to abandon nightsoil methods and not to eat the nasturtiums. Amir still pretends to despise him but suspect they smoke hubble-bubble together in the shed at night.

New development – I have become Wise Woman. That is, by popular demand, dispenser of aspirin, diarrhoea mixture, quinine, sympathy and laxatives. So many camped out at the landing to catch me when I went ashore, have arranged to see them once a week in a room in the bazaar. Thank heaven for French doctor – aged, drunken old fellow, remittance man of many years. But at least can turn to him when it's beyond me.

You must miss Howard terribly. (Can't think what I'll do when Robin has to be 'educated'.) H. writes such long, grown-up letters now! He knows more about Egypt than I do. One day, I do hope, you'll lend him and he'll come . . .

Journal, May 2nd, 1921

Zaghlul returned to Egypt. Strongest attack so far on Milner Commission. Says if negotiations fail Egypt will fight like Ireland. Dread to think what this means – there have already been attacks on Europeans and not just the British. Robin cut another tooth . . . the Sudan's going to be the bone the dogs go to war on, so says old Dr Legendre. No idea how much he was worrying me about Alex. Tonight, thank heaven, back home. But so thin.

3rd May. Frightful row with Alex. Can't bear to put it down. Forbids me even to correspond with Nayra or Ahmed. Don't know him like this. Ran into garden in my nightgown. Big moon. Sand looks like snow. Saiza came after me with a shawl. Still shivering. Heard jackal bark . . .

The telephone woke Charlotte.

'Leo! Sorry. Went to sleep at the desk. Where are you? Are you all right?'

'Luxor.'

'Terrible line. What's happening?'

'God knows. Curfew. Nothing flying. But it's quiet. Tried to hire a jeep. No luck. Just have to sit it out. What's going on there?'

'No problems at all. Miss you. Leo?'

He was cut off.

7

'You must thank Max. I did not wish to discuss the affair and really I know very little about it. But since he insists.' Nina wore her version of a sailor-suit. Striped matelot top, flared white trousers, a red bandana. By daylight, her skin looked lizard-loose, as if she might slough it off. 'I hear you are going to Philae. So much better when it was underwater.'

'I'm looking forward to it.'

'Ruins should be left to fall. This poking about in the past.'

For a moment Charlotte was not sure if Nina was talking about Philae or the Duncan case.

'Well, I suppose there is no harm. Besides, there is very little I can tell you. If I do not then Max will bribe Masoud and Masoud will tell. I suspect that is how Niki got his information about the Duncan daughter. Not that I imagined Niki had a piastre to bribe anyone.'

'Oh – I don't think . . .'

'Well, I do. You realise the silly boy's in love with you? Anyway.' Nina took a breath. She sighed and seemed to make up her mind. 'Of course, you must understand, I was very young, hardly more than a girl. I daresay you have worked it out that I am twenty years older than Pansy Duncan but from what I hear she has let herself go quite pathetically. Have you seen her yet?'

'No.'

'I advise you against it. There is nothing to be gained. Well.' For a second Charlotte thought the old woman had gone to sleep, then Nina's eyes snapped open, monkey-bright. 'You can have no idea what it was like then. The time of the murder, I mean, 1924. Horrible. Two years of so-called independence. A British bungle which gave the Egyptian *barbares* their own little king and reserved everything they really wanted for themselves. Dreadful old Zaghlul making trouble as ever and your Allenby so weak, he had only himself to blame. The French have always been so much better at Empire because they have no morals.

'So. I do not care to understand politics. What it meant to us was violence in the streets of Cairo, friends murdered. All that nonsense about the Sudan as if anyone could possibly want such a horrid country. You know, in the old days, when I first came there with Fahmi, Cairo was a beautiful city? Every morning the boulevards were washed. And Alexandria was quite cosmopolitan. Such fun. We did have fun though I don't believe Fahmi's family approved.'

'Phoebe Duncan — '

'Oh yes. Such a nasty business. I never met her. That would have been November? December? About the time they assassinated your Lee Stack, the Governor-General of the Sudan.'

'November 1924.'

'Yes, of course, you will have looked up your history. So I don't really know what I can tell you. I know we wintered in Beirut – Fahmi was always so sweet, he took such care of me, he wanted to get me out of Cairo. Beirut, now there was a wonderful place. But you were asking?'

'About Phoebe.'

'Quite pretty, I believe. But a silly girl. You English will fall in love with Egypt, an eccentricity I have never understood. And for her, in her position, quite inappropriate. I said to Fahmi, it is the husband I am sorry for. Those Hazims were notorious trouble-makers, the brother and the sister. I think perhaps at the time of the Stack killing the brother was wanted. But I forget.'

Charlotte could see that Nina's attention was wandering. Soon she might get bored.

'Something in the letters makes me wonder if after independence Alex Duncan was doing secret work in the Sudan.'

131

'A spy? Ah, now that is more interesting. In the war, in Cairo, it was fun counting the spies. I was quite naughty. I would bring them together to the same parties.' Nina leaned forward to rap on the window-pane. The gardener had been sitting smoking under a tree. He got to his feet, but slowly.

Charlotte said: 'So I was wondering if Alex might have been the intended victim. He was away so they killed Phoebe.'

'I suppose that is possible. There was gossip at the time. So many theories.'

'And yours?'

'The *crime passionel*. If I were you, my dear, I would look nearer home. The Hazim man.'

Charlotte was startled. 'Ahmed?'

Nina nodded. 'One understands he was handsome. Unmarried. Your girl with revolution in her head, time on her hands.'

Charlotte remembered Phoebe shivering in the garden after the quarrel with Alex, the jackal's bark.

'But Alex forbade her to correspond with the Hazims.'

'And can you imagine she obeyed him?'

'No.'

Nina shrugged.

'So there you are! A vengeful husband. Or a lovers' quarrel.'

'Who said this? Where did the gossip come from?'

'All Cairo. Except for the British. They put up your famous wall of silence, so boring. Not a squeak. And then what does the husband do? He runs away to India.'

'Alex could never have hurt her. He adored her.'

Nina pulled down her mouth.

'In marriage, if there is passion, there is always the possibility of murder.' Nina clapped her hands. 'And now we shall have tea and talk of other things.'

Charlotte looked at her watch.

'I'm sorry. I'll be in trouble with Adila if I miss the coach.'

'Oh, of course, Philae, you poor thing.'

'Thank you for talking to me. I'm very grateful.'

In parting, Nina kissed her cheek.

132

'You are too young for all this dead stuff. And I am too old. Take care.'

They went to Philae. By coach to the landing, then by water, jammed sweatily together beneath the inadequate awning. The outboard engine complained, moaned, puttered into silence and for five minutes, until it was coaxed and bullied into life again, the only sound was the Arabic exhortation from the skipper, which might have been a curse or a prayer. So they drifted in the furnace of afternoon heat. The water was so clear it seemed lit from below and at its margins, granite outcrops and islands cast calm, rose-coloured reflections. No one spoke, though Marietta gave a little puff of pleasure. Max took a sip from his water-bottle and nodded.

On the island Adila assembled her chickens in the full sun.

'With the building of the first dam Philae was for much of the year beneath the waters. To save it from drowning by the High Dam the temples were moved, stone by stone, to this island. Philae was dedicated to Isis and we proceed now to her temple.'

Charlotte strolled in the shade, from time to time catching glimpses of the others following in Adila's train. The water, the stones, the light, a brutal-looking desert beyond – all seemed in perfect juxtaposition, one to the other. In the reliefs she saw the faces of the gods defaced by Copts, the graffiti of Napoleon's army under Desaix. The stone inscribed to the memory of the men of the Heavy Camel Regiment who lost their lives in the Sudan. Killed in action. Died of disease. Waiting in the temple, Max had said, for boats that never came.

Then Charlotte was outside again, resting against a pillar as the small birds she would remember from all the temples discussed their affairs. She saw lantana and acacia, picked a sprig of mimosa and, thinking of Leo, longing for him to be here, heard a pebble disturbed behind her.

'Max.' He looked well today, eyes bright.

'So you too are running away from Adila.'

133

'I look it up in the guide when I get back.' Charlotte smiled. 'This is the most perfect of all. I don't know why. Poor Adila. I'm afraid I'm a very bad tourist. She must have found Leo much more rewarding.' Sitting down beside him, she put her hand on the warm stone. 'It seems silly now. I thought they might be having an affair – Leo and Adila. I pretended not to mind though I did. Now I don't believe they were. But I realise I would have cared very much. This is a funny time, isn't it? Not exactly a holiday. Being cut off, I mean. Somehow out of life. I just hope we're not expected to pay for it.'

'Hal has a remarkable gift for getting credit anywhere he finds himself.'

Charlotte nodded.

'Oh dear, look. Adila's lost her crocodile. She will be cross.' The others, too, had broken away and were wandering or sitting, by themselves or in couples. Only Hal remained by Adila's side. She was talking vehemently and he appeared to be comforting her.

Charlotte said: 'You're looking so much better.'

'Yes, today I am very well. Do you think Adila is crying? Is that a handkerchief? I don't suppose you have binoculars?'

Charlotte laughed.

'You *are* better. Are things going well with Joseph?'

'You could say so.' Max pointed with his stick. A sturdy black beetle was circumnavigating the tip of his shoe with the air of a housewife going shopping. Charlotte remembered the scarab ring she still wore, the talk with Masoud in Hal's garden the night of their arrival. The boy who came from the scarab beetle, wept and created mankind. There was something pleasing about the reminder, as though life really were a circle. The geometry of God. Max was saying: 'That is, I am done with Joseph.'

'You're happy about that?'

'Yes, I am. At last. And Phoebe?'

'How funny,' Charlotte said. 'I haven't thought about her all afternoon. This place, I suppose. And I nearly didn't come. Yes, I hope by the time I'm finished here I can lay her

134

to rest. Not quite yet.' She looked out across the water. 'Was that island the original site? You've been here before, haven't you?'

'We came twenty-five years ago. It was underwater then.'

'With your wife? What was her name?'

'Ruth.' Max adjusted minutely the angle of his green-lined sunhat. 'A Moabite, as you might say. Not of my faith. Many Jews fall in love once in their lives with a Gentile abhorred by their mothers. The difference was, I married mine. I remember Ruth chose to fancy that, looking down, she could see figures moving under the water, looking up. So one might speculate that we were the drowned, the underwater world the real one. In fact, it must have been the reflection of the rowing boat.'

Hal was calling.

Charlotte said: 'What is this temple?'

'Trajan's kiosk. Also known popularly as Pharaoh's bed.'

They stood and Max turned to Charlotte. He spoke with an odd formality.

'Will you allow me to thank you?'

Charlotte did not ask what for. She touched his hand then kissed him on the cheek.

In the air above a falcon lazed on the thermals, wheeled away as a ghost of a breeze came up, ruffling the water. Then it freshened from the north, blowing in their faces as they puttered back, combing the desert into waves.

Charlotte thinks of calling Niki's room, decides against it. He'd be sleeping off last night. Too late anyway for their trip to the bazaar. And perhaps she is postponing what might prove a disappointment: the meeting with Pansy. If it really were Pansy. Instead, she will stay on the island. Leo might call again. Hal has heard (where?) that the situation in Cairo is normalising. Charlotte flops on the bed. She channel-hops on the television from the in-house movie (*Out of Africa*) to the news in Arabic.

135

Stone-faced Mubarak steps from his limousine. Charlotte is fascinated by his bulk, which appears not fatty but muscled as though underneath the almost-too-perfectly fitting suit (with a faint sheen, like Masoud's), he were corseted in iron. An officer salutes. So maybe Hal was right – Mubarak has cracked down.

It is still light, not so late, after all. Charlotte pulls on a thin jacket and goes out into the gusty wind. The plants have been watered, the grass raked, the invisible gardeners have gone. She walks down to the river, past the empty sentry box and finds the tall gates unlocked. She slips through.

Phoebe is busy. She is making her life, consciously giving it a shape and purpose, aware that inaction could become lethargy. And perhaps there is a deeper motive to this ordering of her days: a need to take charge of her own life? The girl who fell in love with Egypt has become like a younger sister, just as the bride has become a wife, a woman. Letters home are less regular. Journal entries not always dated, sometimes full, often a few sentences in dashing writing. The longer entries coincide with Alex's absences. She keeps the journal in a locked drawer.

Journal, Aswan, spring–summer 1921

A. brought me the most beautiful string of ivory from Khartoum. Penitent about our quarrel. Made up, of course. Neither of us mentioned the Hazims . . . if he knew how I hate having something we can't ever talk about but that's how it will have to be. His prohibition makes me all the firmer. No question of giving them up. So this will be my secret. Poste restante not safe (Alex often picks up mail himself) so have made arrangement with Dr L. to be my letter-box from Nayra. He suspects love affair, I'm sure, but v. French and discreet about it (I pray!). Told him it was mail for clinic a nuisance to have at home.

Most painful thing deceiving Alex. And though he can't talk about it, seeing him torn in two. He's not like the others.

Remember him riding with Ahmed in the desert and the
four of us happy together. Knows the Egyptians much better
than I ever could but has to stick with tribe or be destroyed by
tribe. That's what things have come to and will get worse
. . . Having to act against all his natural inclinations making him
ill. Much worse for him than me. Sleeping badly this last
time he was home. Nightmares. Shouted once so Amir burst
into bedroom in the middle of the night with a knife until I
calmed him down. Funny if it weren't so awful – Alex reaching
for his pistol, Amir with knife literally in teeth and me in nightie
and it was all because of a dream . . .

Aswan, November 1921

My dear Howard,

You must *not* let the others tease you or not let it get you
down. An Egyptologist is a fine thing to be and you will be one,
I'm sure of that. They're just jealous so perhaps you'd better
pretend you want to be something very ordinary and boring
and keep the truth secret. Your secret and mine. When you
are grown up you will come here to dig and make a wonderful
discovery – perhaps in the Valley of the Kings. There is so
much still to be excavated. And I shall be very proud of you.

No, I'm sorry, darling, there are no elephants on our island.
There might once have been thousands of years ago – the
old name is Yebu which was Egyptian for elephant. But that
would have been before the desert came. Someone told me it
might have that name because traders used to come here
bringing elephant tusks from Ethiopia. I have my own idea –
when I have sailed past the island in a felucca I've noticed the
rocks looked like elephants lying down. (Here is a photograph
to paste in your Egypt scrapbook.)

Did I tell you there is an old story that the god of the
cataracts lived here and made the first man on a potter's
wheel?

Robin the Ug Monster is pulling at my leg so must go
or he might bite my foot off with his three teeth! I *do* hope
you'll like Stoddards better soon. How awful they read your
letters. Please don't take any risks smuggling mine out to
the post-box. Best of all to make a friend. And when it's really
bad I think the thing to do is pretend in your head they

137

are a tribe and you are an explorer come to study them (the Ugs perhaps?).

A big hug, darling, write to your old aunt soon . . .

Charlotte walks quickly at first. The palms and green cultivated plots are lush but the narrow passages between the houses confusing. She loses sight of the river. The village closes in on itself, plays tricks. She can make out neither the way back nor on to the southern end where Phoebe's house had stood. She is aware of being watched as though the painted houses had eyes. She turns. A woman pulls her veil across her face, a hobbled goat grazes. She has come full circle to the same house with the brass knocker in the shape of a woman's hand. Someone plucks at her sleeve.

November 1921

Dearest Dorothy,

. . . my favourite month of the year. Still hot but the air so clear and bright before the beastly khamsin sends us all mad.

Just as well Mother can't see me now! (Please explain long silences mean nothing more sinister than that I am busy. It's not in my nature to do nothing.) So to get about in the hotter weather kitted myself up with a baladi just like the peasant women wear – wide sleeves, rounded neckline quite low, wonderfully comfortable and cool. And have had my hair cut short as a boy's – Saiza sighing at every snip of the scissors. And here's a joke. Cairene she may be but insisted I kept my lost locks safe in my handkerchief sachet. For a while couldn't get her to say why then she confessed to fear of witchcraft against me! So solemn I couldn't tease her.

Every month plan a trip to Cairo and either there's too much to do here or Alex is away. But hope we'll really make it in December. Meanwhile at the 'clinic' almost every day (followed by good scrub at home with Lifebuoy soap – ouch). Have got really fond of old Dr Legs. So-called by me because Legendre is much too boring and bourgeois and respectable and he has legs like a heron. Thank heaven for him though. Alone, all I could manage was castor-oil, aspirin and sulphur powder. Thought I might be able to help pregnant women just with a few sensible tips on diet and hygiene. To some degree have got them to trust me but learned soon the midwife is regarded as a sort of witch-doctor and was trying to turn them against me.

Dr Legs does have authority though (perhaps an honorary witch-doctor himself) and when he cares to use it they do take notice. Not that there's much even he can do about endemic bilharzia and glaucoma. They might escape the liver-worm if only they'd stop bathing in and drinking the Nile water, especially from stagnant pools. Can you believe it – Dr L. remembers the building of the Suez Canal! His father was an engineer so he spent part of his youth there. Apparently the British were dead against the whole project, which I hadn't realised. And the loss of life among the workmen from accidents and fever was appalling. I asked him if that was what decided him to become a doctor but he gave me the old French shrug and the *je ne me rappelle plus*. Get the impression he doesn't think much of the British. That would have made me cross once but feel differently since I've seen how some of our administrators behave. Or rather, their attitude – as if the Egyptians were children who can't think for themselves and have to be humoured and scolded. Privately, I suspect they're often laughing at us.

So my main job is to coax Dr Legs into staying sober long enough to tell me what to do when we have few real medicines and hardly any bandages and dressings at all. (Even what not to do – am terrified of killing someone off.) Hope to raise some funds when and if we get to Cairo.

What a long epistle! Only because I don't know when I'll next have a chance. Do you and M. really keep my letters? (So does Howard, he says, but that's different.) Perhaps then they're not too boring and when I'm a very old woman I can read them again and remember.

Am writing separately to Mother about all the things she wants news of: Robin's weight, consumption of imported Cow & Gate, number of teeth, latest profound remark. Also trustworthiness of servants (total) and how much I miss England (not a bit).

Except for not seeing you all —
My love as ever,

Phoebe

Charlotte had thought to push a bag of boiled sweets in her pocket but when these are all handed out the Nubian children still persist. Not threatening exactly; nor are they chattering like the cheerful Egyptian children of the countryside, but following as in a game of grandmother's footsteps without the fun. Their clothes are dusty, sometimes ragged. Some are pathetically thin. Snot runs from their noses unchecked. A black-eyed girl fingers her jacket, takes her hand and it is all Charlotte can do not to pull away. They are an obdurate reproach. 'Hotel?' she says but they do not understand or they pretend not to understand. She quickens her pace but the faster she walks the deeper she finds herself in the maze of painted, baked mud dwellings. At last she has to admit to herself, she has lost her way.

Cairo, December 1921

Happy Christmas, Howard! Only time for a postcard. See picture of Continental Savoy Hotel where your aunt grows fat as harem lady on turkey, all trimmings and pud. Hope you are having lovely day with same to eat but snow not sand. xxxxx That's kisses for everyone and extra for you. Aunt P.

Journal, Cairo, December 1921

Five days of showing off Robin – the wives almost inclined to let me off for producing something they can cluck over. Which has given me chance to put in pleas for clinic. So far promises only. Must do myself up 'proper' and set out on begging campaign.

Lovely picnic in desert with A. – stolen time all by ourselves and magic just like old days. If it could always be like this, so easy and peaceful. At least made me feel everything really *is* still good between us and whatever happens nothing can hurt or change that. A. more or less said that . . . was sorry work had kept him away and run him down a bit. Rode back slowly to hotel and skipped Forbes's party (another black mark!). If only Christmas could be like this – plus Robin and Amir and Saiza. But so many invitations. Hope old crêpe de chine still

140

fits. Can hardly walk in high heels any more. . . . Today
A. working as he will be most of time. Last night I asked who
was he reporting to? Casual question. The Mamur Zapt, he
says, as though I didn't know that means head of Secret Police.
Shopping today with Rosemary Gilchrist until I thought my feet
would fall off. Then too many cakes and too much Cairo gossip.
Felt as if I were impersonating the person she wants me
to be till face ached with smiling and neck with nodding. Keep
thinking they haven't changed at all, I have.

At least Rosemary G. helpful with my fund-raising. Quite
practical too. Says must call it Charity. Tomorrow we work on
list of likely victims. She will give tea-party on my behalf.
Horrors! But will stand on my head if it helps.

. . . Horrible. Hate lying to A. but only way to see Hazims
was secret meeting. And if they're watched terrible risk I
might be reported too. So into one taxi to the Qasr al-Nil to
give appearance of respectable shopping, into new department
store buying gloves I don't want, and out at the back into
pre-arranged closed carriage. All the way out to Giza where
Turkish woman (a poetess apparently!) has house she lends
without asking questions. Nayra and I embraced and both burst
into tears like silly girls. Then laughed and both talking at
the same time after a funny awkward pause. At first nothing
about the Wafd but photographs of Robin, Nayra exclaiming at
my poor old stubbled hair and asking about Dr Legs and
Aswan. Presents for Robin and a book for me. Paul Valéry's *Le
Cimetière marin*. Probably shan't understand a word – N.
always imagines I am as at home in French as she is. But made
her write in it and treasure the inscription: *To a friend of
the heart and of freedom*. Don't deserve this and almost howled
again. Then Ahmed came in (still so good-looking but tired,
I thought) and seemed shy. Wondered if he was afraid of telling
me too much, if he knew about Alex's job, but in the end
we had a good serious talk, all three of us. He's got so
grave, much too solemn for a young man and the opposite
of the crazed Arab revolutionary. He was with the Wafdist
leaders at the talks in London last year. Fell out with some, I
gathered – those who wanted to go along with the terms
and to keep them from the female Wafd. So I should think,
says Nayra and he pulls a face and complains: you see how

141

my big sister bullies me. He says protectorate will end but
not the battle.

Nayra announced that was quite enough politics. Talk
lighter. Ahmed seemed to relax a bit. Remembered when we
all had our photo taken together (who took it? Amir?),
the four of us in the garden at Heliopolis. Nayra said one day
we'll all be together again. In Paris, maybe. She would throw
off the veil, dress at Chanel and write a novel. Alex would be
ambassador and I would give famous salons every Thursday.

What about Ahmed, I asked.

I think I'll be an Osiris, he said.

Didn't understand. Then he left and Nayra explained. That
was what the ancients called a dead man – an Osiris.

> *Continental Savoy, December*

. . . so, Dorothy, latest report from Cairo jungle finds animals
just as I left them. Alex says a few new faces at Sporting
Club but pecking order unchanged. Guesses he is a bit *déclassé*
having left military for civil and gave very funny description
of ritual on Golf Links (will save that for later when more time
to write). Truth is, they can't *quite* look down on him because
a) he is so generally liked and absolutely not pushy (and
couldn't care less if anyone did look down their noses) and b)
known to be a favourite of Allenby's.

Women even worse probably because they don't have jobs,
also too much time to think about who's cutting whom and
where their standing is in the barnyard. Climate gets them
down, they're badly dressed and insular and worried about
their complexions, children in England, children here, etc.
Good number turned up for Rosemary's tea-party for my fund,
mostly to get a look at poor Alex's crazy wife, I suspect.
All took their lead from Mrs Forbes, who is still Top Hen and
had decided to be gracious for the afternoon. After my short
speech (me wearing dullest frock, hat and white gloves) she
pledged all of £5, which meant even those who could give
more, won't.

Of course, this isn't fair. There are kind, good-hearted
women among them, they often manage on little money, all the
time trying to put aside enough to educate children, buy
the home they dream of in England. That's the trouble – their

lives are provisional. They don't even want to know Egypt and
do their best not to see it. For me Egypt has become home.
Hope to live and die here – so thankful Alex feels same in spite
of work problems. Though miss all your dear souls . . .

Journal

Bad news. Zaghlul Pasha deported to Seychelles. Such fools.
This will make agitation worse not better . . . Xmas Day some
fun with Robin before we had to go out. Wafdist Women's
Committee protest letter to High Commissioner. Had to stick
on smile when all I want is to go straight to Nayra.

Boxing Day. Said I might take taxi or horse-cab Gilchrists'.
Short meeting with Nayra. Says women planning mass meetings and protests. Daren't stay long. N. upset too because
Ahmed talks of following Zaghlul which would be utterly
pointless when the fight is here. Hate leaving her like
this. Brief words with Ahmed. He's an old man in the cause
and yet still so young, capable of impulses. Perhaps helped
persuade him. At the end he took my hands and said
so seriously I was their good friend but must run no more risks
on their behalf. In return I made him promise to ask if
there were ever a time when I could give help. Though what
I could do from Aswan, I don't know . . . This silly
Eastern thing. Wanted so much to kiss his cheek as I would
Nayra's but instead we have to shake hands . . . pray
that seeing them has not got them into further danger (or
A. into trouble) if I've been followed by bloodhounds of
Mamur Zapt.

All this sounds so absurdly melodramatic. Doesn't feel like
that. Just sad.

27th December To Giza again. Nayra sick but couldn't get
message to me in time. Persuaded Ahmed to stay a little. He
said shouldn't we have housekeeper in but pointless to worry
about chaperone since meetings with either of Hazims must be
secret anyway. Rash, I suppose, but who will ever know?
He promised not to go to Seychelles. We discussed politics a
bit stiffly then suddenly he stopped being shy and we talked so
easily about everything under the sun. Felt I'd broken through
some barrier and now we are real friends.

We left separately for safety. In taxi I thought how funny
– anyone not knowing might take our meeting for lovers' tryst!

28th December Last night 1 doz. white roses delivered to
room – no card but can guess. Told Alex I'd ordered them. He
teased me about secret admirer.

New Year's Eve. Dressing for ball. A. says suddenly, would
you like to go home? England, he means, not Aswan. Just
sat with the hairbrush in my hand, mouth open. Then he kisses
me. See his face in mirror. He says what we both want will
come, perhaps quite soon. Not to ask questions. But if I should
be in touch with the Hazims, warn them. That's all. Then
all togged up we go in to see Saiza bathing Robin. Feel close to
A. again. This will be a happy New Year.

Suddenly one of the children laughs and tugs at her hand and
Charlotte sees the absurdity of the situation, as if there were
anything to fear from children. So she follows where they lead
and there is the river again, the path, the iron gate. The sun
is setting in a sky the colour of dull silver. The north wind
has gathered strength and as the guardian at the gate, about
to lock up, lets her through and shushes away the children,
it blows full in her face, ruffling the tops of the trees.

8

By morning the compliant palms were dipping their heads to the south, rattling their leaves. That was the first thing Charlotte noticed when she slid open her glass door. Then she saw that the wind was slapping the surface of the river into grey waves.

In spite of the rising khamsin, Max still felt unusually well. It passed through his mind that this might be the lightening before the dark, then he put aside such thoughts, shaved with extra care and decided for once to go down for breakfast. Something he chose not to analyse had happened yesterday at Philae. He had thought, of course, of Ruth and how they had seen the old temple still submerged on its original site: the pillared shadows, the trick of water-light by which it was possible to imagine that one saw a figure flitting there between the stones, looking up at them in the other world of air and heat.

But yesterday nothing had happened, yet on the island with Charlotte Max had had a sensation of time taking a long blink so that for much longer than one afternoon he had experienced what could only be called transcendence. As though he had looked down and seen them all, the little figures moving around the island just as once Ruth had fancifully imagined the shadow-man in the drowned temple.

At breakfast in the Orangerie Max spooned up his yoghurt, refused coffee, decided today he would go ashore.

'The Fatimid Cemetery perhaps. A small devotion to Sayyida Zeinab, the granddaughter of the Prophet. One is, after all, related.' Charlotte smiled, Bizz and Fizz looked puzzled. 'All sons or daughters of Abraham. Who like so

145

many of our prophets is held as righteous by the Islamic brotherhood.'

Charlotte said: 'Don't forget the yellow cow.'

Max wiped the corners of his mouth with his napkin.

'Ah, yes, the cow!' He grinned wickedly, looking over the tops of his spectacles.

'What the hell cow?' Hal asked.

'Flaubert's. Also the cow of Moses.'

'What you talking about, Max? God, I hate breakfast.'

Max replied almost primly but the corners of his mouth turned up.

'In the words of the Koran, Moses answers. Lo, he saith: Verily she is a yellow cow. Bright is her colour, pleasing the beholders. No. I am wrong – gladdening the beholders. Well, I shall make my first call at the travel agency. Jerusalem next, I think. If Allah permits.'

Max trotted off. Hal shook his head and took his leave, too.

The others looked out at the swimming-pool. There was a strange muddy light over everything. The loungers and parasols had been put away.

While Charlotte watched, a forgotten plastic chair was snatched up by the wind, tumbled for a yard or two and dropped. The poolside bar was shuttered. A door banged, kept banging. Perhaps by contrast, there was something peculiarly desolate about the scene. Upon some abrupt command the sunbathers had been banished, the pool spoiled. The sun, dully glimpsed from time to time, had taken on the colour of the moon.

As Niki and Charlotte stepped out of the hotel the yellow, sand-laden air slapped her in the face, took away her breath.

Elephantine, March 3rd, 1922

. . . and so I had to write just this brief note to share with you both news you will have heard already (and long before this letter reaches dear old Woking). On the 28th last month the formal declaration was published ending the British protectorate! Yes, Mother, I know you won't approve but this does not mean the Empire is falling down or England

146

sinking. Haven't yet seen the details but as far as Egypt
is concerned this is a wrong righted at last. It makes me happy
and if you can't understand perhaps Dorothy can and will
explain . . . On to things that really matter – Robin's cough
quite better. If he dies of anything it will be of Saiza spoiling
him to death. And Amir guards him like a watchdog as he
does all of us.

Had good talk the other day with one of the gardeners
on Kitchener Island. You'd never believe what they grow
there – and the birds! Have no idea what half of them are.
Gardens there a tribute to Lord Kitchener's enterprise (sent
to India for some of the plants – there's Empire for you,
Mother!). But a lot too formal for me. A General's garden.
Everything in its place, so you feel the flowers will salute
like soldiers. Nothing like my muddle and I know which I
prefer.

As I write the window slams and even before the clouds
arrive and the wind comes up, I know we're in for the
khamsin. That and the midsummer heat are the only times I
think maybe a wet day in Woking wouldn't be so bad . . .

Afraid we may have to postpone leave, Alex so busy
(in Cairo now) with the implications of independence. Latest
portrait of Robin enclosed, best I could do with my box
Brownie. Quite the little pasha now – lord of the bath as you
may dimly see. Has caught some Arabic from Saiza and calls
me Om as often as Mama.

To my own dear Om, salaams and all love,

P.

Journal, March 5th, 1922

Indoors, shutters bolted against wind so it seems endless
night. Hate these sandstorms. Gets in everything. Eyes.
Mouth. Brain. Low patch. Times like this feel everything
pointless. There'll be coughs and desert sores at the clinic
when we open up again and nothing much even Dr Legs can
do.

Last week waited with Dr L. two hours and no one came.
Got Saiza to ask in souk and seems some local shaikh must be
jealous of us and causing trouble. So long trek round to
persuade women to return. Men still staying away. Nothing for

it but myself to see Shaikh Omar who will probably refuse to
talk to female person. So then it will be the even more difficult
job of getting Dr L. to visit him. And so on . . . May have
to wait for Alex to intervene. He has a way with these people,
unusual for a member of the tribe – a matter of humour and
patience and something else I haven't managed yet. Probably
never will. Seems to be a male thing.

6th March. Disgusted and ashamed. Alex back from Cairo.
Reserved points in declaration mean our troops will stay and
we hold onto the Sudan. So many powers reserved it's not
independence at all. As king, Sultan Fuad will be puppet
. . . Only good thing – A. and I had proper talk even tho' he
was tired. He's gloomy about future. Tharwat Pasha's govt.
not representative . . . there'll be continuing trouble from
Wafd. Neither of us mentioned Hazims. He said something
like: you realise I have to do my job, I'd so hate us to
fall out – we can't take on Egypt's troubles. And you mean so
much to me. Everything. A warning perhaps but the gentlest
one.

   Lay awake long time. Sand gets in everywhere, even
through mosquito net. Shutters rattling. Poor little Robin shut
indoors three days now. Khamsin must blow itself out today.
Kept thinking round in circles . . . all this seemed so
simple, a matter of obvious justice when I first came to Egypt
and met Nayra. All so complicated now.

   If you ever read this, Alex darling, I want you to know
that I am sorry I have been an embarrassment to you. Hope I
never do anything to hurt you. Perhaps you love that very part
of me that makes me a black sheep. So if I didn't care
for the Hazims and for Egypt, I would not be myself and we
would not love as we do.

'Cover your mouth.'
   Niki steered Charlotte across the main road in the direction
of the souk. The sand was gritty between her teeth. It was
in her nose, her ears, her eyes. It was invisible and yet the
air was full of it.
   She pulled her scarf across her nose and mouth. She
noted an improbable department store among the Corniche

148

buildings. Niki seemed to have forgotten the theatrical scene the night of Nina's party, his absence yesterday. Charlotte felt sure that if she were to challenge him, he would be astonished.

For a second she could not get her bearings. The Corniche was virtually empty. The weather had banished even the importunate calèches.

She had to shout against the wind: 'Which way?'

'Here. Hold onto me.'

So they plunged into the souk.

In 1923 the Duncans take home leave. For several months there is no correspondence and little in the way of journal entries. Letters from Woking to Howard at school. One, out of chronological order, written from Aswan in December 1922 but included in the package for 1923.

> . . . So this year we'll see you at last and you will meet your Ug-cousin. About last autumn's Valley of the Kings discovery of the tomb of Tutankhamun – Uncle Alex met Lord Carnarvon in Cairo though not to know him. He came out for his chest after a motoring accident and caught the Egypt fever by which I mean what you and I feel and Uncle A.
>
> But do you realise, darling, you share a name with the true hero, Howard Carter? That *must* mean that one day you will come and find things just as wonderful . . .

The two months of summer leave, from June 1923 until early August, are spent largely with Phoebe's mother and her sister Dorothy at Woking and Bembridge. There is also a trip to London and a week in Scotland with Alex's father. In a letter written on the voyage, Phoebe speaks to Dorothy mostly of family matters.

> *Port Said, 1st September, 1923*
> . . . Especially a treat to be with you all at Bembridge on Howard's birthday. Can't believe he's 10! How the years have run by. He's so sweet-tempered and thoughtful. Then just

as you are thinking he's almost too serious, he turns out to be pulling your leg. I know you worry about the only-child thing and that he doesn't mix easily with other children but there's another side to that, too. I mean imagination, sensitivity, curiosity. His drawing. And very patient with Robin, who beside him seems like Attila the Hun. So boisterous I hope he didn't wear you all out. Was thankful to get away from Scotland before they started shooting things!

Bless you for your leaving present – the Katherine Mansfield short stories. Gobbled them down the first day out and then re-read them slowly. She is such a wonderful writer, isn't she? Writes with such clarity and eye for detail. I'd read *Bliss* but *The Garden Party* even better. Wish she published more.

So here I am with K.M's England in my head. Then I look up and decide that is not heat-haze on the horizon but the coast of Egypt!

Journal, Elephantine, September 1923

This really is home. Any reservations dispelled by absence from it. Dear Saiza burst into tears, Amir beaming. No chance to see Nayra in Cairo but letter c/o Dr Legs. Everyone thankful Zaghlul freed and back from Seychelles. But Wafd don't trust new government . . . Alex talking about getting police guard. Hope I can convince him against. Teaching me how to handle revolver I have no intention of using . . . Do understand dangers in Cairo or even Assiut where they're not so accustomed to Europeans. But absurd to imagine anyone in Aswan would hurt us . . .

Journal, December 1923

A. says if Zaghlul gets into power there'll be trouble and if he doesn't there'll be trouble. That is, about the reserved clauses. *Wish* I could talk to Nayra. Her last letter said women's Wafd committee don't trust Zaghlul to stick out for control of Sudan. Or for women's rights. She herself always says extreme feminists confuse issue. Nationalism should come first. Trying to understand these politics makes me realise how naive I still am . . . Robin still coughing.

150

What a month! Gilchrists for Christmas. Realise Rosemary
not so bad. Even though she does raise eyebrows at almost all
our primitive ways, quite brave of her to mix with the likes
of me at all, bearing in mind disapproval of Top Hen. But
Geoffrey really the most idiotic little man. Refers to R. as the
Sitt – meaning wife, which makes her sound like his camel.
Been cross, I suspect, ever since he failed to get India posting.

In middle of Geoffrey booming, Rosemary being tight-lipped,
worry about Robin's cough, if it was bronchitis. Frantic search
by Amir for Dr L. missing presumed drunk. Meanwhile new
cook produces not Xmas dinner but sulks. Finally hysterics no
one could calm. Saiza gets from her at last that jealous sister-
in-law has used magic to make her infertile and daughter she
had before aforesaid infertility developed fever and bleeding
after circumcision. Rosemary appalled in proper female way at
last hideous custom but can't understand why I can't just issue
orders to stop it . . .

Wafd government voted in.

Missed two periods now. Told Alex. Agreed if a boy,
Andrew after his father. If a girl, Violet or Pansy . . .

In the narrow streets of the bazaar the scent of spices mingled
with the taste of sand. Charlotte caught glimpses of rich, dark
interiors. Because of the storm little was on display outside
but voices called after her, grinning youths ran out in front of
her, she could hardly keep up with Niki's long stride.

'Here, I think,' Niki said. 'No, round that corner. Yes, this
should be it.'

'But it's a shop.'

'Above the shop, I expect.'

So now there was the shopkeeper to be tackled, who
appeared, politely, in Arabic, to be explaining that alas, he
knew nothing of a white woman. Duncan meant nothing to
him. He wagged his head sadly.

'Got any money?'

'Yes.'

Charlotte handed over a bundle of notes. Niki put them
down on the counter. The shopkeeper's memory returned.

How foolish of him not to remember! He even recalled that
he spoke English. His father had worked for the British in
Ismailia. Of course, you will be wishing to see Om Kabira!

'Yes. Om Kabira.'

Yes, she lived upstairs. Yes, he would take them. Past
an overflowing lavatory, through a small store-room, up the
stairs.

'There she lives. But she is *souvent malade*.' He knocked
on the door, ushered them in. 'A good woman,' he said. 'A
mother to us all. My mother. Om Fayoom.'

The woman lay on the divan, heaped with dusty cushions.
Her body looked water-swollen. The room smelled of cat.
The shutters were closed against the khamsin and for a
moment Charlotte could not be sure if Fayoom's knock
had woken her.

'Please forgive me. I hope you don't mind – '

This was one of Pansy's better days. Her voice was clear,
light, pleasant, faintly amused.

'No, you must forgive me. A visitor. English!'

'My name is Charlotte Hamp.' She introduced Niki.

'Come here. Sit closer. Don't be afraid. I'm not as
old as I look.'

Couldn't be more than her sixties, Charlotte calculated.

Fayoom's wife brought tea. Niki folded himself into a corner.

Pansy was saying: 'I was asleep you see. I was dreaming
of someone else. You look so like her photograph.'

'Phoebe Duncan?'

'Yes. My mother. But how – '

'That's not so surprising. I'm Howard's daughter.'

'Howard? You must wait for me. I shall remember.'

I shouldn't have come, Charlotte thought.

'Are you ill? Can we help?'

'No, no. Thank you. These are good people. They could
not be kinder. I don't often get visitors. I forget how long
I've been here. Forty years or so, I suppose. Papa died, you
know, then I had to wait for the war to finish.'

Pansy's fingers were swollen. The rings cut into the

152

flesh. She wore a man's-sized kaftan and a shot-silk turban. Disguising baldness, Charlotte suspected. Pansy closed her eyes. For a second Charlotte thought she had gone to sleep. Niki whispered: 'I'll be off then. You can find your way back?' Charlotte nodded. As Niki shut the door behind him Pansy opened her eyes.

'And then I never wanted to go to England. A cold, wet place. Well. So you're little Howard's daughter.' Now Pansy had made the connection she seemed unsurprised. 'It is good of you to visit me.'

Charlotte wanted to say: how can you live with them if they killed her?

Instead she asked gently: 'Can you tell me anything about her? Phoebe, I mean. I've been reading. Journals. Letters. She loved Egypt so much, didn't she. And the way she died, that was awful.'

'I never knew her, of course. Father had the photograph, the one like you.'

'You disappeared. There was a story you'd come here. But after India no one was sure what happened to you. I'm not tiring you?'

'No, no.' Pansy was remembering. 'All my childhood I had this idea of Egypt, of wanting to come here. Sometimes in India Father talked about it. He felt exiled, I think, though after that awful business he had no choice. There were those journals and papers. At first, he used to lock himself in his study. I felt sure he was reading them. Once I thought I heard him crying. He was drinking too much by then. The servants would say: your father is not so well, you must be quiet. I've been very happy here. All these years. I had never expected such happiness. Howard's daughter, did you say?'

'I really think I should go.'

Pansy appeared not to hear.

'The servant saved me. Amir. He hid me in a cupboard. I dream about that cupboard sometimes. Though I could not possibly remember it. But you are young. All this will be boring you.'

Charlotte shook her head.

'Did you see the journals? Any of the papers?'

'No. Father just told me one day that he'd packed them up and sent them off to England. To little Howard, who would not have been so little by then.'

'I have them now,' Charlotte said. 'Would you like to see them?'

'I think not. Too late.'

A shutter banged. Below, in the street, someone called.

'I must go.'

'No. There is a question. You have come to ask.'

'It doesn't really matter.'

'I believe it does, to you.'

'Well, I have a feeling some of the papers are missing. I've been trying to find out. I know what happened that night but not why.'

Pansy seemed to be making up her mind about something. Then she heaved up her great bulk in the bed, scattering kittens, and with her stick hooked out a metal box from under the bed.

'There. Open the box. In the big envelope. Some Father either missed or didn't want anyone to see. I found them after he died.'

'Are you sure?'

'Take them, take them. I know them by heart. No use to me.' Pansy sank back on her cushions. She clearly had difficulty in breathing. 'This wind.' Then she said something in Arabic. Then: 'Please would you be good enough to leave me. Ask Fayoom to come.'

'Can I see you again? I would so much like to help.'

'Very kind, my dear. But I've made my life. I'm at home. That's enough. Now if you would call Fayoom.'

Charlotte folded the envelope double and put it in the inside pocket of her jacket. At the door she paused. She had the feeling that Pansy had already forgotten her. It seemed an intrusion to press further.

'Can I ask you? What was the real reason you never

went to England? Even to see Phoebe's people? The family?'

'Because England killed her.'

All Charlotte remembered was that she had been utterly lost. The sand in her eyes, the labyrinth of narrow streets – like the Nubian village, but this time no child took her hand to lead her.

One wrong turning, then another. Midday perhaps. Or the shops had put up their shutters against the ever-rising wind. Brightly coloured cotton garments were snatched like handkerchiefs from an outdoor rack, flung down, picked up again, whirled away. A stink of dung in the suffocating wind. The busy souk emptied. The sound of a radio – where? In a doorway, a bundle of rags. No, a beggar, hunched, legless, blind eyes turned upwards, rattling a can, calling the everlasting name: Allah!

This was the other Egypt: the one Charlotte had sensed that first night in Cairo. All the rest – had it been no more than skin-deep?

(Her hands hurt and her face. She felt the sting of iodine.)

Turn here, surely. But it was a blank wall, dead-end. A goat crying. Turn again, run. The flip-flop of plastic sandals gaining on her. Black faces, narrow skulls, boys calling. The rattle of pebbles brought back the shock of the stone in the temple of Luxor but this time she was alone and purblind with sand. A limping dog crossed her path. Absurdly she noted a bald patch on its flank as though a huge thumb had crudely rubbed off the fur. Above her head an unseen window slammed. She could even hear voices quarrelling, yet she knew, as a dreamer does, that if she hammered on that door there would be no answer. The sand fell like secret snow, turning the slippery ground where slops had been thrown, mud-red. Her shoes and feet were red.

Out of breath, Charlotte ducked her head, glanced round. That might have been a shape, a boy? Two boys? A dervish thrown up by the sand? Then the shout again in the language

155

that sounded so often like a curse – both trilling and brutal –
and Charlotte ran and fell.

'There,' said Marietta. 'Now you'll be absolutely fine, dear?
Does the iodine hurt? I guess the worst of it was done when
you fell. Your poor hands. Now you have a nice sleep.'

Charlotte felt as if she were watching a film. She sat calmly
up there in a corner near the ceiling and looked down upon
her body on the bed. She could even see the small, touching
bald patch on the crown of Marietta's hennaed head.

'I feel stupid.'

'That's the pill the hotel doctor gave you.'

'Oh, yes. I think I remember. And falling.'

Hal said: 'Max found you outside the Coptic church. Just
as well he was there.'

'Ah. Yes, I do remember.' Charlotte half sat up. 'My jacket?
Where is it?'

Marietta said: 'In the cupboard. There are some papers in
the inside pocket. But I'm afraid you lost your bag. Or it was
snatched. Now, dear, let the pill work. Hal, come on.'

'Please? I'd like to see Max.'

'Egypt,' she said. She had woken an hour, a day later, she had
no idea, groggily taken a shower and gone back to bed. With
Max had come tea, very sweet, a sprig of mint floating on top.
'D'you remember the French girls? They were frightened on
the road from Dendera, in the dark?' Charlotte reached out
her hand, winced. Apart from the cuts, every bone in her body
ached. 'Sorry, I'm not making much sense. Have I thanked
you? For saving me?'

'You have. Perhaps you shouldn't talk.'

'I want to. I want to know what happened.'

Max shrugged.

'I saw nothing.'

'But I was stoned?'

'It seems so. Unlikely in Aswan but possible in the present
circumstances.'

'But who?'

'Local boys high on sheesha and Fundamentalism? Students up from Assiut? The khamsin – everyone goes a little mad. I doubt if they meant any real harm. Or if they did, they wouldn't have carried it through. You were only about a hundred yards from the Corniche.'

Charlotte sank back on the pillows. It was easier to talk in this aquarium light. Max sat in one of the armchairs. She was glad of him.

'It sounds silly,' she said, 'but it's something I've been aware of ever since Cairo. The Egyptians so friendly, yet something about Masoud, for instance, about all of them. About the whole country – a feeling that there's an invisible curtain. Something even Phoebe never understood. I think she knew it. That the light dazzles you but on the other side of the curtain there's a darkness. Just being a tourist perhaps? The foreignness? More so here than most places. I'm talking too much. I'm sorry.'

'No. No, I've felt that. Wondered how much Joseph did. Coming from the desert, the life of hand-to-mouth, into that Pharaonic certainty. Well, a different story.' Max said suddenly: 'Most tourists are untouched. They look. They go away.' The familiar gesture, raising his spectacles, rubbing the bridge of his nose. 'There have been new arrivals, bearing the *Herald Tribune*. It appears the revolution – if it ever existed – is off. Egypt is mobilising at Suez. The age-old trouble with the children of Israel in Sinai. Hal's faith in Camp David is touching but romantic. Sadat, I fear, was an interlude of unreality. There seems no end to human madness, criminality. Anyway. Time for my exit, I think. To the not-so-tender mercies of my own tribe. Perhaps that's what it's all about: tribes; tribal ritual, pride, envy, tribal subdivisions.'

Charlotte nodded. The abrasions on her hands, from falling, hurt more than the bruises and cuts from the stones.

'I suppose Phoebe tried to belong to two tribes at once. Can't be done. Remember Forster? Fielding and Aziz at the end? The horses swerving apart? You know, I forgot to ask Pansy if Phoebe had a love affair with Ahmed, if she knew.'

157

Max finished his tea, put down his glass.

'I shall be sorry to miss the ending. If you find one. Now I must let you rest. Shock's tricky. It can catch up with you.'

'I wonder,' Charlotte said. 'We lead these little, self-engrossed lives. But they're so fragile. Then there's a shock. It needn't be Egypt. I think in a funny way I'm glad I had that shock.'

'I wish you weren't going. I wish there'd been something I could do for Pansy. She really has gone native, as Nina said. I felt the intruder. And I'm certain she'd have it no other way. Would you be very kind and open the curtains? Before you go?'

Journal, Aswan, April 1924

. . . Don't know who to believe. Nayra writes Zaghlul's government weak on the Sudan issue, avoiding confrontation. Alex says things are pretty awful and will continue so as long as we insist on British control of Sudan. Ever since he forced independence issue Allenby attacked for weakness – makes life even more difficult for Alex because he sees both sides . . . History makes me feel cold, small. Such a strong wind, nowhere to hide. Dear old Dr L. He says no such thing as history, only politics, in which no sane man would indulge.

Picture of Dr Legs the other day (as I'll always see him). Sitting at rickety cane table on his verandah after clinic, glass in hand, wearing straw hat so old it's half eaten away as if donkey had chewed it. Verandah sagging under weight of vine he fails to tend. Assorted cats, mostly mothers with kittens, which remind me I'm six months gone and according to Alex, Mother, Dorothy, Rosemary G., etc. totally irresponsible for refusing to lie down indoors with feet up stuffing myself like an ortolan. Even more thoughtlessly eccentric for exposing Pansy/Andrew to hideous disease.

Dr Legs pulls his long yellow moustache and says I am exceptionally healthy young woman and pregnancy is not an illness. He lights a stinkweed Egyptian cigarette, coughs, calls for more wine and when we've done the local gossip, relates splendid tale of the surrender of dreaded foe. Shaikh Omar who had scared away so many of our 'clients' – all the men and some of the women – believed himself to be dying and sent for Dr L. who refused to go. So his Shaikhness has himself carried here after dark and calling upon Allah, Mohammed and anyone else he can think of, submits himself with gritted teeth and closed eyes to the ministrations of the infidel.

Much head-wagging and solemn French mutterings on the part of Dr L., poking our Shaikh with his long finger where he knows it will most hurt. Privately diagnoses constipation. Prescribes not castor-oil, which they all know of, but the strongest laxative in his western pharmacopia. Two days later son of Shaikh appears with many gifts. After seeing death-pangs father miraculously healed and preparing this moment for a pilgrimage of thanksgiving to Mecca. Thus our reputation higher than it's ever been and our only problem is to cope with the flood of the new faithful.

I tell Dr L. my secret plan to stay for this birth in Aswan. Feel it will be an easy one and with his help and Saiza's determined to stick it out.

He nods as though this were a perfectly normal thing. Then Amir presents himself to take me back across the water to the island. But we sit on for a bit, talking about nothing in particular. Books, reading. Dr L. has a great library, mostly heaped in piles anywhere there is a space. Moths and beetles have got at some of it. Offers me Wallis Budge's *Book of the Dead*.

Suddenly strikes me – I ask him, has he ever written? Not really, he says – not with that hypocritical self-deprecation but casual acceptance that nothing he does will be of any true importance (think he'd be horrified if it were). I laugh, push a bit. What is not really?

Then he delivers in halting English, translating as he goes from the French, in turn from the Latin, a mediaeval poem about a man contented in his small house, grapes on vine, etc. Says it's Petronius Arbiter. Very short. Perfect. About living in a small, good place, wanting to die there. They say only miserable people are drunkards. Not true.

Looking down his long nose, says he has dedicated his life to attempt to teach his parrot Latin. Mission defeated by servant so all it can say (in Arabic) is meatballs and beer . . .

Darling Mother and Dorothy,

Alex will have telegrammed you the news. Pansy six weeks
old now and looks just like her name – face like a flower.
I'm tired but very well, all the better for getting rid of Scottish
nurse from Cairo. Sister Sinclair, v. sniffy about attending
birth in such outlandish place but though she wouldn't admit it
could see she was impressed by Dr L.'s midwifery skills. She
insisted whole house scrubbed with carbolic. Dear Saiza quite
put out by her presence but happy again now we have Pansy
to ourselves. Any fears I had about Robin (jealousy, feeling
left out) dispelled. He's decided Pansy belongs to him. Have to
watch him like a hawk or he'd have her out of her crib
and cart her round like a puppy.

Please believe we're safer here by far than we would be
in Cairo, where I agree there is some trouble, though not half
as frightful as you might have heard by rumour. You must
not take notice of half-baked travellers' tales and newspaper
reports, invariably exaggerated . . .

. . . Alex home for a whole month, so except for you
two and Howard, have all I want and love in the world in this
one small place. Alex took me, tenderly as if I were made of
egg-shell, across the river to the western bank (me demanding
an outing). Just at my favourite hour of day, late afternoon,
when everything still, a reddish-golden light at this time of year
and we saw long train of camels with riders going off into
desert. To us looks as featureless as sea, yet the invisible
tracks they follow are like roads to us. Shall never cease
to wonder at that. Can honestly say, if I knew I were never to
leave, to die here, I would be happy . . .

It took Charlotte several minutes to realise what had woken
her. The silence. The khamsin had blown itself out.

That night Max Stiller died.

9

'In his sleep,' Hal said.

Charlotte was helping to clear up Max's room. The body had been discreetly removed by the backstairs.

'So little, I think we can get it all in one grip.'

Charlotte found the empty pill bottle by the bed.

'We don't say anything about this, do we?' Hal shook his head. Charlotte slipped the bottle in her pocket. The bed had not yet been stripped. There was still a dent in the pillow where Max had laid his head for the last time. Charlotte touched it. 'I thought he was ill but it must have been worse than I imagined. Suppose I'd better take the manuscript – the Joseph book. Track down his publisher. He'd have destroyed it if he didn't want it published.' They were finished. 'I'm glad he went, for his sake. But I'll miss him terribly.'

Hal nodded. 'A sweet man.' He looked vulnerable, more shaken than Charlotte would have expected. Woken early by the chambermaid, he had had no time to shave. He said wearily: 'You know of any family? There's the papers to fill in, the arrangements.'

'I don't think he had anyone.' So that was it, of course. Poor Hal. 'You mean the body? He didn't want to be buried in Egypt, I'm pretty sure of that. He was going to Jerusalem but London would be fine.'

'London then. I'll get down to it. You'd never believe, Charlie, the complications of transporting a corpse.'

Charlotte said gently: 'He did have us, Hal. He was happy here.'

Before she left the room she smoothed the pillow.

*

161

The BBC World News announced that two prominent Pan-Arab Nasserites had flown to Belgrade. There was still uncertainty concerning the identity of the instigators of the recent local disturbances in Egypt. The country now appeared to have been restored to normal. The curfew in Cairo lifted. The number of Europeans formerly rumoured to have been injured greatly exaggerated.

There was a message from Leo. Luxor airport had reopened and he hoped for a flight the next day.

Charlotte's body still ached and her hands were sore. She sat out on her verandah for a while, her face in the sun. Except for the grittiness between her teeth and the sand in her canvas shoes, nothing remained to remind her of that strange sandstorm of the mind the khamsin had brought. The Nile smiled, giving back once again the precise reflection of the desert bluff on the opposite bank.

Now she went inside and took Pansy's fat envelope from her jacket pocket.

First a yellowed cutting, so brittle it threatened to crumble between Charlotte's fingers, reported the 'cowardly assassination' of Sir Lee Stack, Sirdar of the Egyptian army and Governor-General of the Sudan, in a Cairo street, 19th November, 1924.

> . . . the killers made their escape in a taxi. Your correspondent voices the hope of the entire British community that these murderers will be brought to justice summarily and without mercy. Also that the High Commissioner, before handing in his resignation, will take stern and forthright action.

Here, near the end, Phoebe's writing is spiky, thinner, as if she were running out of ink or using a twisted nib.

> *Journal, Elephantine, November 1924*
> They've done it. Poor man. And Allenby will be blamed as usual for being soft on the Egyptians . . . So late, tired, all I can think is what will this mean for Alex, Nayra and Ahmed.

All mixed up with worry about that cough of Robin's come back. No temperature but keeping him indoors. Alex caught me crying today and was so sweet I just cried more. Can't write home in this mood. Sent message to Dr Legs, apology. Couldn't manage clinic. Must stay for Alex, anyway. Ordered to Khartoum so will miss Cairo funeral.

. . . Made up my mind today – no more fuss. Alex off in the morning. Talked all hours. Hope he understands why I refuse to go to Cairo. Hate to think of danger to him in Sudan. As for the children and myself – there are shadows but the people here are my friends. Safer here than on that awful train (and with Robin's cough). No one will hurt us. Must trust.

For first time Alex all but admitted he has been working as agent (spy, that is). As though I ever believed he was just a policeman! What this means, he says, is that we are all in danger – he has put us in danger. Poor love, what rubbish . . . Promise to sleep with revolver under pillow (no intention of using it). He's the one I fear for. And the Hazims. In this mood don't care tuppence about political justice. Only that those I love will not be hurt.

The chambermaid knocked and Charlotte took the papers out onto the verandah. One end was in shade. She could hear the shush of the invisible gardeners. A party of tourists were sailing by felucca to the Island of Plants (Kitchener Island to Phoebe). Life had returned to normal.

The remaining journal entries were mostly undated, some cryptic, interspersed with jottings about everyday matters.

Note from Nayra via Dr L. She asks and at same time says I mustn't take risk. She's distraught and no wonder. No way of getting Ahmed out through Alexandria or Suez so if I can find him somewhere. He'll come some time in next few days or not at all. Thank heaven Alex away . . . If you ever read this, darling, forgive me.

Must work out what to say to Amir and Saiza if I have him here. And get word to Dr L. in case he goes there. To land in dark on western bank away from guard . . . Today Robin coughing less I think. Dr L. came, let him play with stethoscope and listen to his own chest. Funny, he's always a favourite with small ones. Treats them like people, not toys, and disreputable not a word that means anything to children. Some kind of hypnotic authority about him so even Robin becomes angel . . . He agreed to help. Knew he would. When I tried to explain held up his hand. What he doesn't know he won't have to hide.

Suppose I shouldn't be writing this down at all – held in evidence against me etc. But can't burden Dr L. and need to think it out. . . . odd how small things keep one's sanity. Saiza just come in wanting menus for day but really to deliver latest in our continuing domestic dramas – the Nubian who already had wife and two children has summoned entire family including two grandmothers and goat. All installed in garden shed! And such a sweet letter from Howard today. Told Saiza we were having a visitor and she was not to speak about him, to tell Amir too. Quite simple after all. Might have known. Their loyalty absolute though I don't deserve it . . .

Charlotte lay back. Half the morning had gone. There in her hand was the letter from Howard, dated September 1924. Her father was now eleven. She looked into his dying eyes full of things unsaid and felt close to tears as she read.

Dear Aunt Phoebe,
Thank you for your letter. I am glad you are well. I am very well. So is Granny and Mother.

I don't mind much this time about going back to Stoddards because I'm older and there are lots younger than me. Please don't worry about whether I'll be all right. Am taking back my tortoise for the Pets' Corner. Doesn't have a name yet. We've got a new dog at home Granny says is a handful. I am not doing too badly in Latin. The weather is not too bad.

Lots of love,

Howard

Charlotte went to the poolside bar for a snack. Marietta was sunning herself, a kitchen timer by her side.

'Though at my age, who cares? So good, dear, about your lovely husband, you're quite better now? You have just the skin for melanoma, you keep in the shade though they can do wonders in Australia they just whip off the lesions, so clever. You remember Sydney, Ed? So we'll all be leaving now, isn't that sad?'

Hal was not sun-bathing. He sat on a bar stool drinking whisky glumly.

'Got to get back to the Consulate. Then Egyptair. The Ancients had nothing on the funerary rites of Near Eastern bureaucrats. Sorry, you call it Middle, don't you. I tell you, Charlie, don't die in Egypt. Had a shot at getting Max to Jerusalem but they don't want dead Jews.'

Charlotte realised that she had never before seen Hal unshaven. His stubble was white. It seemed a long time since she had considered him a man entirely comfortable in his skin.

She pushed aside her sandwich.

'Where's Niki?'

'Left this morning,' Hal said.

'But I don't understand. He didn't say. Where's he gone? Why?'

Hal managed a grin.

'Because Leo's coming, I'd guess. To Khartoum.'

'He said he might but I never believed him. You know Niki. But there's a war in the Sudan, isn't there?'

Hal nodded.

'Also an expensive hotel where the best black-market plutonium deals are made.'

Charlotte heard her own laugh, sharp. There was a shout from the pool. Bizz and Fizz.

'But that's absurd! Niki! Whatever does he know about plutonium?'

'Enough.' Hal got up to go. 'Who wants to buy. Who wants to sell.' He shrugged. 'Or maybe he's just gone to be a Dinka.'

Walking back to her room Charlotte remembered Niki not being able to swim. Standing by this very pool in the dark. She remembered the conversation with Max about tribes. Niki, she supposed, never had one. She remembered that

165

odd, good day in the garden of the Old Winter Palace. The sub-dialogue. He had been such a tentative presence, hardly more than a ghost.

It was too hot outside now, even in the shade. Charlotte switched on the air-conditioning, undressed, quickly shower-ed, slipped on a thin robe and settled with Pansy's papers on the bed.

At her side she had her own notebook. In the first few pages there were ordered queries, references, dates to be checked, historical points. Then nothing until the scrawled notes she had made since they arrived in Aswan. Questions rather than notes.

Motives – Alex spy, killing reprisal. Phoebe not intended victim?
Anti-British murder gang?
Nina's crime of passion? Would explain Pansy's remark about her father's state of mind in India. Possible but unlikely.
Amir or the Nubian? Someone she trusted? Working for whom?

The light through the curtains really was eau-de-nil. Inside her room, Charlotte could not be seen but she could see, passing the window from time to time, pale shapes like shadows thrown on a screen. In the aqueous green light, the colour of garden shade, she read.

Evening, November 25th, 1924
This morning Dr L. sent his boy with message to say our visitor arrived. Landed from felucca just after dark, dressed as native boy. Put him in Alex's dressing-room at the back – if trouble best way to run from there and only Amir ever goes in that room. He's tired and hungry but so pathetically grateful . . . insists only one night or two at most. Seems they escaped in taxi. He might have done better to lose himself in Cairo but has been on police list so long his face known. Anyhow, couldn't stand life on the run. Hopes to get out of

166

country and regroup with others to work from abroad. Or, the border being so close, to disappear into the Sudan. Dear A. He's still so young yet he's done this terrible thing. Looks as if he has fever. Hands trembling like an old man's. Worried about family. I gather Nayra questioned but not held. She disapproved of what they did, it seems, and they've always been so close that hurts him most. Perhaps because he knows she was right . . .

Morning Dr L. over. Such French discretion. Not a word about our visitor but at pains to chat to the guard. Brought me fuchsia cutting, lingered smoking over coffee giving general air of everything ordinary. I'm wonkier than I'd thought. Could hardly bear to let him go. Seeing him leave, felt really alone. . . . Robin much better and only too lively. Escaped Saiza's clutches and ran around in his pyjamas. Awful instinct of children made him suspicious – why Alex's room locked. Got him back to bed in the end but all this makes me feel I have done something unforgivable. . . . Have never been thankful before for darkness coming so early. He'll go tomorrow, and night must be safe.

Can I really depend on Amir and Saiza? It's asking a lot because it means in a way they are betraying Alex. And the other servants, no idea what they know, what they think. There is a shadow but I must trust . . . Read Robin his story from *Jungle Book*, helped Saiza bath Pansy. Have put Robin to sleep in my room tonight, he's so restless.

Changed for dinner. Ate with difficulty swallowing in solitary state. Talk afterwards with our visitor in the dressing-room. At first he was stiff, polite, then I took his hand and he blurted everything out. He had helped to plan killing but when it came to the point – the deed – hated being part of it. And the awful thing, he said, is it's got us nowhere. Things will be worse for everyone. Allenby will have to go and there could be no other Englishman the Egyptians respected as they did him.

Still haven't taken in implications of what happened next. Shall destroy this tomorrow. I put my arms round him meaning, I think, to be maternal though now not so sure. And he embraced me, then we were kissing and it all seemed

167

natural and right. He needs me more than Alex has ever done but it wasn't just that. He loves me, says he has always loved me since he first saw me. My own feelings so confused, hoped writing it down might help. Can never speak of this to anyone, not even Dr L., never Nayra. And, of course, it must stop now, here.

Late. Writing in bedroom by Robin's nightlight at the escritoire we found last summer in Alexandria.

Can't sleep. Air so still, every sound sharp. Jackal barking. Yamani doves disturbed, complaining. Someone in the garden –

Then there was a typed envelope, marked strictly private and personal, to Captain Alexander Duncan, Srinagar, from the office of the High Commissioner Lord Lloyd. Charlotte took out the handwritten letter, dated July 1925.

Dear Duncan,

I have the unofficial permission of our new High Commissioner to convey to you certain facts which may, I hope, throw some light on the tragic events of November 26th last year. I imagine you may already have your suspicions that the findings of the coroner's court and the court of enquiry did not amount to the whole truth.

Bluntly, I suppose you would call it a hush-up . . .

Charlotte read on. It was an awkwardly written letter but these were awkward truths. Publicly, what the writer called the indiscriminate murder gangs operating against British targets had been allowed to take the blame. In fact, 'the agents of whom you know' had been after Ahmed, the 'notorious terrorist' for his suspected implication in the Stack murder, and traced him to Assiut then Aswan: 'where, it appears, your wife gave him shelter. Or possibly he entered the house unknown to her and was hidden by the servant Amir.' The killers were hired.

Charlotte bit her lip. So that was it. The authorities had feared the making of a martyr, a gift to 'these vicious revolutionaries', so Ahmed Hazim was to be done away with quietly. To disappear.

As so frequently happens with these Arabs, matters got out
of hand, Hazim made his escape and in the darkness and
confusion the outcome was what it was. At least we can be
thankful to have caught and brought to justice the six assassins
in the Stack affair. Though we were sure of it, Hazim's
part would have been difficult to prove and, given his name and
reputation, to hold him and bring him to trial would certainly
have called down more trouble on our heads.

Poor Phoebe. Those later stolen meetings with the Hazims
– all had been noted in the reports of the Cairo Secret Police.
They were 'ill-chosen friends' and Phoebe's only crime 'was
naiveté and ignorance of the danger of such associations'.

There was a postscript instructing Alex to destroy the
letter and to impart its contents to no one.

The letter concluded:

My dear Duncan, if I could undo what has been done, I
would, gladly and with all my heart. As it is, Rosemary sends
her warmest wishes and we both hope that you and your
daughter may make a new life in India. A posting I envy you
although it must be said that we all feel safer here since
we have a man with a firmer hand on the reins than our former
High Commissioner.

I trust this letter will not deepen your grief.

It was all the most infernal bungle.

Yours, very sincerely,

Geoffrey Gilchrist

Charlotte sank back, the letter still in her hand. The
complacency, she thought, the hypocrisy. There came into
her mind the terrible and pathetic box of secrets Nina had told
her about, the Bocca del Leone on the wall of the governorate.
In a way, you could say it was a secret that had killed Phoebe.
Phoebe writing by a child's nightlight, hearing the slap of bare
feet in the garden. Locking the bedroom door, taking Robin
in her arms (while Amir snatched Pansy from her bed and hid
her in a cupboard, so now she was a woman living or dying
in a room that smelled of cats and dung and spice). Were

169

there shouts? Did Amir call to Phoebe? And while Ahmed slipped out through the dressing-room window – perhaps to find a concealed boat or to swim to the western shore – the intruders smashed their way easily into the wooden house. Had they planned all the time to let Hazim escape? Or was it, as Geoffrey said, an unintended act of darkness and confusion – an accident?

What Phoebe must have felt as she saw the knife which Charlotte imagined, for some reason, to be curved; covering Robin's head.

Begging – she would have begged for the child.

10

'My face,' Charlotte said. 'Bit of a mess. Only scratches really though. What a pair. You and your limp. Does it hurt? Perhaps we shouldn't have come so far?'

Leo shook his head. They were standing on the beach at the southernmost tip of the island. Phoebe's house had been here, a building probably not unlike the present museum-bungalow. They had walked through the Nubian village handing out biros and the children, even when there was no further booty to be had, watched them from among the trees. Always the children. So that's what we really are, Charlotte thought, trippers.

They were on the edge of the dig. Leo couldn't resist it. He bent, picked up a pottery shard, turned it in his hand and dropped it back into the sand.

She had expected something else. To run into his arms? To burst into tears? Only now did she grasp that all the time she had insisted he was safe, there was nothing to worry about, she had been in a kind of shock, living through a little of what she might have felt if someone had come and told her: he is dead.

So there was the odd stiffness between them.

He turned and said: 'Dark soon. Better get back.'

'Yes.'

'Don't feel much like Hal and the others, do you?'

'Not really.'

'You want to see the sarcophagus? In the museum? The mummified ram?'

'No. They're shut anyway.'

*

171

They lay with the giant bed between them.

Charlotte said: 'Did you find what you were looking for? At Gurna?'

'No. A tomb all right, under Old Gurna. But empty. Robbed recently, I'd guess.'

'I'm sorry.'

Leo took her hand. Across the bed their fingers just touched.

'Doesn't matter. I was just bored and worried about you. Needn't have been, need I?'

'Of course not.'

'Poor old Max.' Leo sighed and lay back. He looked thinner. 'Are you finished with Phoebe?'

'Nearly.'

Charlotte lay awake for a long time listening to him sleep. He woke once, mumbling, but she could not make out what his dream could be.

The last morning, they went, just the two of them, to Philae.

Charlotte trailed her hand in the water. Predictably, the engine seized up and they drifted peacefully enough.

She said: 'There was one last letter in Pansy's collection, to Alex. Horrible. Not really a letter. One of those anonymous pasted-up things. Telling him to watch his wife with Ahmed Hazim. I can see why he went nearly crazy in India. That poison-pen thing and hiding the journals, no one to talk to, a secret he had to keep, it would have sent anyone mad. Yet he kept them. I suppose because anything he had left of her was precious. Oh, look, are those egrets or ibis? I never know the difference.'

They landed. At this time of day – early morning – they were almost the only visitors. The weather had settled again. There was a milkiness to the light and a stillness, so it was hard to make out where reflection ended and rock and desert began.

They sat and looked out over the patient water. Leo sprawled, leaning on his elbow.

172

'Last time I saw this it was a heap of dust. When they were moving the temples. No birds. No flowers. Yet it seems to have been here for ever.'

Charlotte nodded.

'I like Isis. She's more human than the others. Mourning for Osiris. She went mad. Then after Horus was born she had to beg for a living.'

'The goddess of last resort,' Leo said. 'The one you could appeal to when there was no hope.'

'Yes. But it's not that.'

They walked for a while until they reached the spot where Charlotte had paused with Max. Leo was standing behind her. She felt his hand touch her hair and turned with a wrenching movement, clung to him, her face against his chest. She could hear herself crying, a harsh and painful sound, animal grief, the tears of crazed Isis.

'What's all this then?'

Leo put one hand on each side of her face until she was forced to raise her head and look up at him.

'I was so afraid for you. I thought you might be dead.'

'Not dead. Here I am.' He kissed her eyes. 'Now. Steady. Mop up?' Leo produced a handkerchief. 'What salty tears.'

'Sorry.'

'No.'

Whatever the awkwardness had been, it was gone. They walked on, arm in arm, then sat in the shade to eat their bread and oranges. They drank from the plastic bottle of water.

Leo said: 'You have no idea how much I love you.'

'I do.'

'But it wasn't just about me, was it? There was something else?'

'Maybe.'

There was, Charlotte thought. He was right. Some grieving that had to be done in the way of Isis; not just for her fear for Leo and the risk one took in loving, but a true, good mourning for her father, for Max. Even for Niki, still alive. And for Phoebe. It was, after all, all right, not entirely

173

sentimental, to shed tears for someone she had never known:
a shade connected to her by blood; dead, more alive than
Charlotte had sometimes felt herself to be.

But now she could let her go?

Someone wanted to go to Groppi's, another to a great little
place for kebab in the Cairo bazaar. In the end they finished
up eating dry pigeon and drinking Coca-Cola in the dark at a
Moslem establishment that was supposed to be very quaint,
near the Manyal Palace. It was cooler in Cairo, there was a
cloud over the moon, but at least it had stopped raining.

Whatever emergency there had been had ended as if
nothing at all had happened. Hal was restored to himself,
Egypt to the tourists who would leave their mark on monu-
ments and temples and tombs; not vandals necessarily,
simply a new race following in the footsteps of Christians
and Moslems and Balzac and W. Stephenson.

Nina and Masoud had joined them on the flight so Hal's
gang was almost complete. No Max, of course. And Niki –
Charlotte saw him in her mind, a figure like a stick insect,
walking away into a dangerous country, diminishing.

'D'you think Niki will be all right?'

'Niki'll be fine,' Hal said. 'Always falls on his feet.'

'Where's Adila?'

Nina pulled a face.

'Meeting another of her package tours. The Americans are
back. And then I suppose it will be those tiny Japanese.'

'I'm afraid we were a disappointment to her. Not very
good tourists.'

After dinner they went back to Hal's villa. Nina patted the
empty seat on the sofa.

'Now tell me, my dear, about your sad lady? Was I
right?'

'Phoebe?' Charlotte sat down. 'Her own people killed her.
That's what it amounts to. You were half-right. Ahmed Hazim
was certainly in love with her but there was no affair. There
never would have been, I think.'

174

Nina's gaze was sharp. Charlotte remembered what Max had said, that the last instinct to go is curiosity. Nina had warned her not to look but Nina now wanted to know.

'And was she in love with him?'

'A little, perhaps. Or with Egypt. I think she got them muddled up.'

'And are you in love? With this terrible country, I mean?'

Charlotte laughed.

'Me? I'm just a tripper.'

The night was warmer than it had been on the trip out and the party had spilled into the garden. Charlotte walked between the roses and this time it was Leo she found by the fish-tank where she had talked with Masoud. About the creation myth, she remembered, and Egypt and her scarab ring, the one she still wore.

Charlotte said: 'I wonder if Alex knew that Phoebe was followed when she met the Hazims, on that last trip to Cairo. He must have done, I think. In a way, I feel sorriest of all for him. He had to live. And that awful poison-pen letter. The killers were never caught so we'll never know if it really was an accident or if they meant to kill her. At least, they were never caught officially. Someone said – was it Niki? – Egypt's an oubliette. Truth is relative to contingency, always, I suppose.'

'And him? Ahmed?'

'Might be alive still. And Nayra. Amir.'

'You could find out?'

Charlotte shook her head.

'I don't want to know any more. D'you understand?'

'Yes.'

She slipped her hand through Leo's arm. Dim shapes were all around them in the garden. Half-formed people, they looked, waiting to be created.

The cloudy air was soft and full of scents. Charlotte gazed and saw the red and green stars of a fat plane thumping its way downstairs. She saw the other ghosts pointing upwards. Then someone laughed with faint shock as the lights indoors where the party had started were dimmed. The room was empty. There was a second's utter darkness then somewhere an unseen hand pulled a switch and the outdoor lamps came on. So the house became the dark place and the garden was full of light.